D1516524

JESSICA SANTIAGO

Palmetto Publishing Group, LLC
Charleston, SC

Copyright © 2017 by Jessica Santiago.
All rights reserved. No portion of this book may be reproduced, stored in a retrieval system, or transmitted in any form by any means–electronic, mechanical, photocopy, recording, or other–except for brief quotations in printed reviews, without prior permission of the publisher.

For information regarding special discounts for bulk purchases, please contact Palmetto Publishing Group at Info@PalmettoPublishingGroup.com.

ISBN-13: 978-1-944313-83-8
ISBN-10: 1-944313-83-4

For my sweet Craig, who always told me unicorns were real. I will love you for a thousand years. I'll love you for a thousand more.

For my Grayson, who changed everything and taught me what redemption is. Nothing I am at this moment would be possible without you. I love you, bug.

For my little Lily Grace, who shows me the magic in everything every single day with her sweetness, innocence, and beauty. I love you, my sweet quirky princess.

And for my soulmate, who always sat proudly by my side at the reject table. I love you to the moon and back.

TABLE OF CONTENTS

INTRODUCTION

ONE OF THE BEST WAYS TO KILL first date nerves is to choose a venue that screams safe space. This safe space happened to serve alcohol, and drowned out the sound of any awkward conversation with pretty terrible live music from the eighties cover band playing on the make shift stage.

"I'm going to get us some more drinks," he said.

"Sounds perfect. I'll be here." I flashed my best smile and bedroom eyes his way.

He laughed, bumped into a table, and walked toward the bar. I watched him walk to the bar then quickly ran my fingers through my hair to give it a little tousle. The crowded pub didn't offer much privacy. There were people everywhere laughing, dancing, and talking over one another. There was nothing particularly impressive about this place. The smell of alcohol pouring, along with the scent of the smoke lingering in the air gave it a certain vibe of despair. It was a typical pub with dull lighting, light colored solid wood floors, dark green walls, and a bar with a shiny wooden surface. There was one small window near the front door; I always felt a little claustrophobic in places like this. I preferred to be outdoors or in larger spaces. Doesn't everyone?

"There you are. I thought maybe you had abandoned me," I said. No sooner did the words escape my lips than I wondered if I were pushing the flirtation thing too fast and furious.

"Not a chance," he replied. Clearly the flirtation was going at just the right speed.

We had a few drinks, did a little dancing, and then decided to take a walk on the beach. I was grateful for the escape. I wanted to be alone with him all night.

"Hold my hand, and walk with me like a gentleman," I said playfully.

"I'll hold your hand," he smiled, "I don't know about the gentleman part." He pulled his hands out of his pockets and reached for mine. He locked his long fingers around mine. My heart quickened a bit when our fingers touched for the first time. His hands felt a little rough, but I didn't mind. We had been walking along together for about a quarter of a mile. The wet sand was making its way through my toes; it tickled, and I laughed out loud.

"I like your laugh."

"The sand is tickling my toes, I can't help it." The sound of the water was keeping a melodic beat for us as we walked hand in hand. We hadn't seen anyone in sight for a while. We were far enough away now from everything that the only light available was the illumination from the beautiful full moon; it lit up the surface of the rippling blue water perfectly. He was babbling on and on about how much he loves the selection of beer at the pub we just left, and how he doesn't mind spending money on a night out with a beautiful girl. He stumbled a bit as we walked along. I offered to tell him a bit about myself, but instead he just wanted to tell me how beautiful I was.

"You have the most beautiful eyes I've ever seen."

I bet he couldn't even tell me what color they are, I thought, and smiled to myself. It was painfully obvious that he does this often, and he thinks he is doing pretty well tonight. I couldn't help but notice him noticing my body in my long white linen skirt, and blue bikini top. My dark hair reached halfway down my back and was bouncing in the wind in big loose curls. The natural copper highlights throughout my hair were catching the light of the moon just right tonight.

We only met yesterday, although I'd been watching him for weeks. Every chance I had I would watch him from a distance. There was something about him that intrigued me; it had a lot to do with his almost effortless charismatic nature. He seemed to command attention without putting any thought into it at all. He didn't come across particularly kind when I would overhear him with his friends; his mannerisms were fun, casual, and gave the impression that life was a little like a game to him. Every time I spotted him he had a different girl falling all over herself pining for his attention. He talked about girls like they were completely disposable and laughed about his conquests to his buddies. It was almost as if his ego was an actual living, breathing creature following him around everywhere he went - a little sidekick tagging along side of him. The thought of that amused me. I typically didn't date blondes, but he was fun and good-looking in an obvious kind of way. He had the kind of exaggerated confidence that you couldn't help but believe. Watching him win the attention of whatever new girl he was with on a particular night was like watching a clever jaguar toy with its prey to manipulate it into thinking he was something else, only to scoop up his victim and devour them.

Neither of us had spoken in a few minutes. He let go of my hand and threw his arm around me. His fingers were sliding up and down my back. I could feel the anticipation building of what was going to happen next. My heart beat quickened; my stomach was in knots. I knew he was expecting something, and it was typically at this point in the evening that I surrendered. That's what they all really wanted anyway, and having all of their attention for just a few moments made me feel unique, powerful, and worshipped - even if it was all pretend.

I gently guided him closer to the water so we could feel the coolness of the ocean tease our toes. I stopped walking, grabbed his hand, and looked up at him. He tried making a joke, but I wouldn't let him talk. I took a deep breath and used two soft fingers to put over his lips letting him know that it was time to stop talking. I put my arms around his shoulders, and lifted myself on him so that my legs were wrapped around his waist. He tightened his hold on me, grabbing onto my thighs tightly - I could tell he was ready for more. He licked his lips.

"I knew you were a wild one the moment I laid eyes on you, Kai," he said. The way he said my name in that smooth and raspy voice of his was extremely sexy. For a moment I hesitated with nervousness. He must have sensed it. He muttered something to me, but I didn't understand him. If I had bothered to remember his name I would have let him hear me whisper it in his ear. I didn't. His breath was warm on my cool face. I kissed him softly, and ran my fingers through his long blonde hair. I could taste the combination of the salty sea air, along with the taste of alcohol that lingered on his tongue. His hands were holding me up tightly upon him. My stomach was tied up in knots of excitement, and nearly ached with anticipation. It felt as if there were a hundred tiny dragonflies fluttering about in my stomach, and tickling me with their rapidly moving little wings.

"Open your eyes for me, I want you to see me." He opened his eyes, looked right at me, bit his lower lip, and leaned in to kiss me again. I threw my head back, looked into his eyes, and laughed as I watched his face wash over with a look of sheer terror and shock when he finally saw me. He was finally looking at me. My eyes must have looked insane with excitement; I could feel them glowing. I revealed my fangs, grabbed him by the back of his smooth neck, snapped my head forward, and sunk my razor-sharp teeth right into his flesh. He tasted every bit as good as he looked. I wrapped my legs around him as tightly as I could, and pulled him under the water with me until I had taken everything he had left. We violently submerged into the water. My long dark hair floated above us like a beautiful dark velvet blanket as we sank deeper into the ocean. The water surrounded us like a big sponge pulling us in. It was maddening in the most wonderful way. I felt so alive, out of control, and beautiful. With one hard push under the water I plunged him towards the tide, and the mighty ocean did the rest for me - just like it always does. I laughed to myself and thought, "Why am I ever surprised that they are all exactly the same? I didn't even have to sing." I hummed a sweet tune and glided through the waves guided by the full moon's hauntingly beautiful light.

CHAPTER
One

MY EYES POPPED OPEN, and I gasped. "What the hell was that?" I said aloud. This was not the first time I danced with this nightmare while I slept. For as long as I could remember going to sleep, I could remember dreaming. My dreams were painfully vivid and I was always capable of recollecting almost every detail. Sometimes they were ordinary enough, when thinking back upon them, it was difficult to distinguish dreams from actual experiences. Sometimes my dreams were extraordinary - full of magic and enchantment, and sometimes I had dark nightmares, like this one. It happened so often that I never thought too much about the dreams, but there was something different about this recurring dream. This dream almost felt like a memory, or perhaps a warning of some sort. I'd have to put it out of my head for now, otherwise I would obsess over it and think of nothing else the entire day.

I closed my eyes again, and listened to the sounds of the waves crashing against the shoreline outside of the window above my bed. Slowly the images from my dream began reappearing in my mind. The colors of the images were vibrant, and the memory of the sounds of his screams, as well as my haunting laughter were as clear as the clanking of the wind chimes outside my window.

My mouth was so dry, I licked my lips and swallowed. What is that taste? I wondered. Salt. I tasted salt. There was something else... something coppery yet sweet. Blood. I tasted blood and salt. Last night's nightmare, was no nightmare. There was a full moon last night, and the water commanded me as it always does with every full moon cycle. Sometimes, if only for a few short moments, I forget who and what I am. Those are my favorite moments, the moments before I am pulled back into the reality of what my life actually is. I never asked for this. I never wanted this. I never would have dreamed that it was possible, but yet here I am. I am what is commonly referred to as a mermaid - only in reality mermaids do not swim around singing, and rescuing people from boats and cruise ships. We hunt...and we kill.

Suddenly, in as much time as it took to blink, everything came flooding back to my mind. I was remembering everything - every detail. I felt sick. My stomach churned. I winced and brought my hand to my forehead. My fingers lingered there for a moment as I traced the outline of my own face. Perhaps one day I would wake up and be a normal girl with normal problems, until that happens, I had to stop trying to forget who I really was. What did I want to be? That question had been presenting itself more and more as of late. There were some things about myself I had very little control over, and this was one of them; I completely transform into a dark and magical creature during the full moon cycle. I embrace my darkness, and I become an altogether altered version of myself, my true self - a powerful mermaid with un-imaginable strength, heightened senses, and a stunning, shimmering tail that could take me miles and miles throughout the waters in the time it takes most mortals to bat an eyelash. A mermaid, perhaps a monster.

Each month I am called to the sea. It's a hunger and a craving that I cannot control. Every fiber of my being pulls me toward her. It is beyond hunger or desire, it's powerful and magnetic. I must spend time swimming under this world I try to be a part of, but don't fit into. I wouldn't survive if I didn't allow myself to be pulled to the water during the full moon. I don't actually need to kill every time I am called to her - I can survive without killing as long as I am in the water, but mermaids are dark creatures and sometimes the craving for lust, blood, and destruction takes over. It is something I have almost no control over. If I leave her embrace during the moon phase, I must hunt and feed on man in order to survive. When I am in the water I am safe. The sea is the ultimate source of life. I need it to sustain my own during the full moon.

I enjoy the hunt; actually, I love the hunt. I stalk and study my victims the days leading to their fate. It's important that I despise them, so that I can enjoy tormenting them. I seduce them, lure them in with the magic of my kind, and ultimately kill them in the sea. There have been times during other lunar phases that I've contemplated giving up the hunt entirely and living out my existence beneath the surface, but I am always drawn to the land - to destruction. It is difficult living with a foot in both worlds. There is an internal battle going on inside of me every day. Mermaids, much like humans, were made of darkness and light. The difference is we are, by definition, half animal and ruled by forces that have been around since the beginning of creation.

I threw my legs over my bed, and slowly rose to my feet. I stopped in front of the mirror for a moment to drink in my reflection. Sometimes I liked the person looking back at me, and sometimes not so much. This was one of those times that I did not particularly care for the young woman looking back at me. I ran my hands over my chest and stomach wondering why any of this was important when it all just fades away anyway - it certainly does for humans. I slid my hands across my narrow waist, and traced the slight curve to my hips with my fingers. My hair was all over the place. It's wild, and wavy. I reached for the brush that I kept on the small white wicker table next to the full length round mirror, and did my best to tame my long dark tresses. My skin is very fair, but with a lot of peachy undertones, my lips are full, and naturally look as if I've just bitten into fresh berries. My eyes are probably my most unique feature; they are bright green with hints of yellow, big, and almond shaped. I stared back at my reflection remembering every step I'd taken up until this point that had gotten me here, I suddenly realized that this year's birthday was a big one - I'd be turning twenty-five. "How could that be already?" I said out loud. It seemed like not so long ago I was only turning eighteen, and coming of age - that's when we turn. We live as hybrids until our twenty-fifth birthday. It is then that we become immortal, and the aging process ends entirely. It was too early in the day for such complex thoughts. I took a deep breath, and shook my shoulders back and forth a few times to try to shake it out. "Enough," I said to myself out loud. "Enough." I pulled off my white cotton tank top and matching panties, headed for the shower, and did what I could to wash my thoughts away. I've always thought you could scrub away just about anything if you stayed in the water long enough.

I spent the rest of the morning walking along the beach and contemplating my next move. The salt in the air was refreshing; the soft breeze lifting my hair behind me felt nice. A group of small birds ran along the water scavenging for food. I watched them for a moment wondering what it must be like to be a bird. Their existence seemed so simple, they seemed so free - yet they were never truly alone. They all flew away together, flocked together.

KAI

I watched them and realized it was time to move on from this town. Having to walk along the same parts of the beach that I had taken countless lives over the past few years was starting to bother me somehow. Sometimes I would envision the sugar white sand turning into a pool of blood, and I'd hear the desperate cries and screams of my victims. Those sounds were becoming deafening in my mind. It was bothering me that this was bothering me, but rather than obsess over it, I figured I'd act on it. I lived a private, and discreet life - and there were no others here like me, so moving on was as simple as diving in the water. It was really that easy. It was time to move on. There was nothing keeping me here, and nothing I needed to take with me. I walked out into the water until I was about waist deep, then submerged under and began swimming. I would swim as far from here as possible, away from all that I had become over the past few years.

The transformation from human legs to my tail always happened in salt water regardless of the lunar phase, but during the full moon my tail would emerge in any body of water. It was not painful to endure, it happened gradually as I entered the sea water. Having my tail form was a feeling of relief, freedom, and pleasure - it was a glorious sight, although not many humans would ever see this, and it was even less likely they would live tell the tale. I glided easily along with the current. My tail gave me the advantage of strength and speed underwater. It was a deep shade of turquoise that was such a natural color, it would seem unnatural to most humans. It almost looked as if it was covered in a kind of magical glistening dust.

The water was glorious and refreshing. It warmed my blood and brought me indescribable happiness. I swam for miles and miles, deeper and deeper into the azure sea gliding along smoothly... effortlessly. I was faster than the iridescent blue, purple, and silver sailfishes that would often try to pass me by. I passed through beautiful underwater caverns covered in limestone, and magnificent caves so far below the earth's surface, most humans will never know exist. I smiled at the beauty of the unique sparkling gems, exotic sea life, and creatures not yet discovered or named by man. Hypnotic and alluring underwater forests and gardens met me at every turn, they were some of my favorite places to visit in the sea. I'd often fantasize about living there permanently…a simple, quiet life under the waters and away from the temptation of land. I could have my own small sea castle built down here, or use an old wrecked ship as the base of my quarters. The possibilities were truly endless. There were so many distinct colors and beauty to experience with every turn. This would be a sensory overload for a human, but for me, it was simply home.

Everywhere I looked there were beautiful red and purple sea stars, tropical parrotfish with their bright colors of blues, greens, yellows, oranges, purples, and reds - amazing creatures that could change their colors, shape, even their genders in a lifetime. The seahorses were peaceful, magical, and clever enough to camouflage their colors as well to protect themselves; they were various shades of reds, purples, pinks, browns, and black. They greeted me peacefully, and let me know I was welcome among them. I swam alongside angelfish, and admired their beautiful stripes of vibrant colors along their bodies and fins. I ran my fingers against unimaginable textured and colored rocks as I swam along, and enjoyed all the magic the sea possessed. I truly felt at home as I took in all the magnificent colors of life in the mysterious and powerful sea. There was never a shortage of wrecked ships or ruined cities to discover. The sea is an enchanting world full of beauty, mystery, and magical creatures - but this was a very dangerous place too. There were sea monsters, dangerous beasts, venomous creatures, and dark beings as well. Nothing is ever truly what it seems deep in the sea. There is nothing more breathtaking than the sight of the sea anemones that are painted beautiful vibrant colors almost resembling underwater sunflowers, yet they are usually waiting for unsuspecting fish to get close enough to be caught in their venom filled tentacles.

I would occasionally stop to rest in a secluded cavern where I would find delicious plants and vegetables to eat. I'd often find myself surrounded by multitudes of fish, sea turtles, and marine mammals acting as guardians to me. Mermaids are one of the sea's most beloved, and worshipped creatures. It is important to keep us protected from harm. We are immortal, but there is no shortage of dark magic users down here that would love nothing more than capturing, and harnessing the powers of mermaids. We were the true daughters of the sea - of the old ones.

I could communicate with all life underwater without actually needing to speak. I could hear their thoughts, and feel what they were feeling. I felt the love from all of them. It was much simpler down here than it was above land. Feelings were straight forward, there was no jealously, or complicated emotions - at least not among most of the sea creatures. There was happiness, love, survival, and a powerful sense of family. The water was something beautiful, and appreciated. We didn't pollute our own environment, or disrespect our world. There was conflict, dark magic, and danger - but always a respect for the bodies of water, and fear of the old ones. I hadn't seen any others like me since I had been in the water, but I could sense that they were relatively near. I had not seen any others like me in many years, and with this being the year of my immortality, I knew it was only a matter of time before that all changed.

After swimming for what seemed like several weeks, I decided to bring my head above water, find a large rock, and bathe under the warm embrace of the sun for a while. The sun can't damage my skin, and its warmth feels good in the fresh air. I could spend hours and hours laying on a rock basking in the sun feeling at one with the water beneath me. The sun's warm embrace, and the peace here was comforting. The complete quiet is wonderful. I don't hear all of the voices screaming in my head, or the call of water driving my thirst - I am just me, whatever that is. It's my serenity. I laid there on my back with my arms stretched out, my hair fanned behind my head as a pillow, and my eyes closed for hours. The light reflecting off my skin and scales was a sparkling sight to behold. Every so often I would smile softly, stretch, sigh, and flip from my stomach to my back. I thought about the water and how it called to me - how it called to my hunger. I thought about how I would spend the rest of my day, and I thought of nothing at all. I began feeling restless. I shifted into a sitting position. I needed something to amuse myself now that I was so well rested, and recharged.

I looked around to determine if I was anywhere worth being. "This looks inviting," I said in barely a whisper. Off in the distance I saw a small remote village on an island on the southern east coast of the United States. It was breathtaking. Luckily, I have been doing this long enough to know that walking onto an island or seaside town completely naked is a sure way to draw quite a bit of attention to yourself, which is something that I certainly did not want to do today. I typically swam quickly to shore, grabbed a towel lying close to the water, and swam back out so quickly that the human eye was unable to detect me. This is exactly what I was going to do right now. This area of the beach was beautiful, and very remote. I could only make out a handful of people along the sand that stretched for at least 5 or 6 miles. I waited until no one was in sight, then allowed my tail to dry and disappear. I stood up, wrapped the towel around my body, and walked along the beach. The first thing I noticed was all the thriving vegetation all along the shore line. There was an amazing backdrop of glorious cliffs that look as if they were brush stroked by the Gods themselves in beautifully painted colors of pinks, purples, and grays. The white sand was so soft it felt as if it were massaging my feet with each step I took. It glistened in the warm sun like it was covered in crushed diamond dust. There were beautiful black horses galloping freely along the sand.

"This is paradise," I thought. I felt strangely drawn to this place, and decided I wanted to explore further.

As I walked along the sand I found a small boutique. It had a small storefront window with beautiful sun dresses hanging, there was also a carved wooden sign that said open hanging on the door that was propped open.

"Hello," I said to the girl working behind the register. There were no other customers in the store. She looked a little suspicious, which I'm sure was at least partially because I had no beach bag with me, or anything other than the towel hugging my body.

"Hi. Can I help you find something?" she managed to say with a smile. I couldn't detect an accent. She sounded completely…. ordinary.

I quickly spotted a simple long white strapless dress on one of the rounders that were displaying dresses. It was made of chiffon, and I couldn't wait to get it on.

"Yes, actually I need to try this on. I plan on wearing it out of the store." The young freckled redhead opened a fitting room for me.

"Sure. Can I grab anything else for you?"

"Ummm, no I think that will do. I will grab a few things myself once I am dressed." On my way in the fitting room I placed my hand over hers and looked into her big chestnut colored eyes. She was frozen.

"I am going to wear this dress out of the store, then continue to shop. Once I finish, you are going to wrap everything up, give me the cash from your register, tell me to have a great day, then forget you ever saw me. Okay?"

"Of course."

I didn't like resorting to magical manipulation, but I had to get started here. I couldn't very well walk around scouting for food, and a place to stay wrapped in a towel with nothing else, and no money. I promised myself I would find a way to repay her once I settled into a hotel, called the bank, had my debit card replaced, and got into the swing of things here. I had more money in more accounts than I'd ever need. I acquired a great deal over the years with my special influence on men, and a little luck meeting a few guys that were great investors. She would completely forget ever having met me, and be no worse off for it, I thought, at least that was how I'd justify this in my mind. The dress fit like a glove. A few pairs of jeans, shorts, blouses, knit tops, bathing suits, undergarments, dresses, shoes, some accessories, and a handbag later, I was accepting the cash from my little shop girl, and on my way.

"Have a great day!" she said.

"Thanks sweetheart, you too," I smiled and waved goodbye. From the time I realized what I was, and acquired my power I had not once taken a woman's life. I didn't plan on beginning to do so today.

I walked a bit further into the town on the island in my new dress, and continued to be amazed by the natural beauty here. There were lagoons covered in Spanish moss, and glorious trees everywhere. The abundance of wildlife was breathtaking for an area that was also populated with humans and residences. There were no buildings higher than two stories, no busy roads, and no traffic. There was one small hotel that looked like a mini-castle on the island. Other than that it was small cottages, cabins, and bungalows. There were small diners, cafes, and boutiques here and there, but it was all very charming and quaint. I learned from exploring the small island that it was called Gray Mist Island for the gray mist that lingered beyond the cliffs on the island in the mornings, and in the evenings. I'd never seen anything like it. I was intrigued. I walked along a bit further to the hotel. It was along the beach with sweeping views, and nestled into a little nook surrounded by a quiet lagoon. There was a wooden walkway that led from one set of the beautiful French doors of the property that wrapped along the building, across the lagoon, and led right on to the beach. There were massive Oak trees, and Spanish moss almost everywhere you turned. I passed a few people here and there, but most kept to themselves. There were a few hellos, but no one seemed to pay very much attention to one another.

"Good evening, Miss," a man said as I walked along to the hotel. He was working outside of the hotel doing landscaping. He looked about forty-five or so, a little rough around the edges, but attractive, with very honest eyes. His eyes were crystal clear blue, and looked as if they belonged to a much younger man.

"Hello," I said.

"That there is the Cliffside Inn, it's the only hotel on the island." I looked at him for a moment, but didn't say anything - mostly because I wasn't sure what to say to him. He seemed harmless enough. He took a few steps toward me, and extended his hand. "I'm Adrian, and you look new here," he smiled. I put down a few shopping bags to free a hand to quickly shake hands with him.

"Is it that obvious?" I laughed. "My name is Kai. I only got in today." I hoped this meet and greet was nearing an end, because I wasn't quite ready to start spinning tales about myself just yet. He took a few steps back towards the area where he was working. I sensed that he wasn't exactly in the mood to make a new friend either.

"The Cliffside is very nice place. It's pricey, but people come from all over to stay and experience the island. Most people rent cabins or villas, but the Cliffside offers longer stays for folks."

"Great, I'm sure it will be wonderful. It was nice to meet you, Adrian."

"Nice to meet you too, Kai. I hope you like your stay here with us," and with that he went right back to his work.

I walked along to the front entrance which was beautiful - it truly did remind me of a magical little stone castle by the sea. It was something right out of fantasy novel. I walked through the large double doors and stepped into the lobby. It was more like walking into the magnificent foyer of a grand stone manor. I guessed it was built in the late eighteen hundreds. There was a soaring formal stairway in the main lobby, beautiful marble floors, stained glass windows, gothic fireplaces, and rich fabrics on the walls. This will due, I thought. I was greeted quickly by a woman at the front desk. She looked about my age. She was shorter than me, I'd guess about 5'5, with straight dark blonde shoulder length hair, a gorgeous tan, and small dark blue eyes. She looked grateful to have a break from the paperwork I noticed her working on as I walked in.

"Welcome to the Cliffside Inn. Are you checking in?" she said in a sweet cheerful voice. I made my way over to the front desk area.

"I actually don't have a reservation; will that be a problem?"

"Of course not," she said as she began typing on the keyboard of her computer. "This is our off season, we are rarely at maximum capacity." I noticed how well manicured her nails were.

"Okay, let's see what we can do for you." She pressed her lips together, and shifted her weight from side to side as she looked for an available room. "How long will you be with us?"

"I'm not sure. There was a gentleman outside that told me you offered extended stays here. I'd like to start with at least 4 weeks."

She looked up at me and smiled.

"That must have been Adrian. He works here on the grounds - we all love him. Okay I have a suite for you. I just need a credit card to reserve the room, and I need you to sign here." She handed me a little blue index card with very basic information to sign. I picked up the pen that was on the desk, and began filling the card out for her.

"I actually only have cash on me. I am waiting for the bank to send me replacement cards. I lost my wallet while I was traveling. Is that a problem?"

"I can make an exception since you will be with us for an extended period of time. No worries. Please just get the information to us when you receive it," she said.

"Thank you so much. I absolutely will."

"I love your dress by the way. My name is Molly, if you need anything at all please let us know. We serve breakfast every morning in the dining room from seven until nine thirty," she said.

I smiled. "Thank you." She handed me my key card, and told me where my room was. I thanked her again, and headed down the lavish hallway, and up the grand staircase toward my room. Yes, I thought, I think this will all do just fine.

CHAPTER

OVER THE NEXT FEW MONTHS I fell into a routine. In the mornings I would wake up, and sit just outside of the grand dining room in the outdoor cabana overlooking the ocean. I would taste the salty sea air on my lips, and read the local paper. Some faces were beginning to become familiar at the hotel, others changed from day to day. This was a barrier island, and while it was not a crowded tourist area in the traditional sense, there was no shortage of travelers here. I mostly kept to myself, and spent the days exploring the island. I would either hunt or swim during the full moon cycle. I had gotten to know a few of the regulars that came into the cabana for meals, and some of the staff. This morning I was interested in sipping my tea, nibbling on my mango chunks, and reading the weekend section of the Gray Mist Metro in peace. Regretfully, this was not the case. Mr. and Mrs. Claude were arguing at the table next to me. I had gotten to know them from their ritual morning arguments day after day. They were both incredibly friendly…when they weren't at each other's throats that is. They were locals, both in their late thirties, and carried themselves like they had enough money to buy the entire island - for all I knew they did. Robert and Rebecca Claude looked like they just stepped off a golf resort welcome brochure every morning. They were both fit, tan, and both wore entirely too much fragrance. Robert had salt and pepper hair, brown oval shaped eyes, a nose that was almost too straight, and a perfectly structured square jaw bone. He came across as quite the ladies' man. I only began observing him because I was considering turning him into prey last month, but I quickly decided not to once I realized he had a wife and family. I do have light within myself three and a half weeks out of the month, I thought. Rebecca was just as beautiful. She was very tall with long curly bleach blonde hair, round baby blue eyes, and a perfect oval shaped face that revealed no signs of her age.

"I'd appreciate it if you would just let me get a sentence in. Don't you ever get tired of listening to yourself?" said Robert.

"How could I when it is all I can do to save myself from yet another one of your insightful lectures, sweetheart?" Rebecca remarked.

"Let's ask Kai," said Robert.

"Oh no, no no no. I am not getting involved in this one," I said.

"Come on Kai, you're a woman, you will absolutely side with me on this," Rebecca playfully pleaded, "I want to spend the day at the spa. He wants to spend the day looking at real estate. What would you do?" she asked. I smiled as I rose from my chair, and pushed it back under the table.

"Neither." I flashed them one last smile before leaving them. "Sorry guys." I could still hear them debating as I walked from the cabana. I made small chit chat from time to time to be polite and to keep up positive appearances, but I was happy to dodge an actual conversation with them.

"Good Morning, Ms. Cordula. How are you?" asked a member of the hotel staff as he breezed past me in the hall way. I see him nearly every morning in his red and black bell hop uniform, and I could never remember his name. They didn't wear name tags, which certainly didn't make it any easier. I flashed him a smile. "Quite fine, thank you." I was on my way out when I spotted Adrian working in the garden. He was wearing a pair of torn jeans, and a white T-shirt.

"Hey, Adrian." I liked Adrian. I spent a few afternoons chatting with him as he worked on the grounds. He would tell me about this plant, or that flower. It was nice. It reminded me of how little I knew about my own father, and how I missed having someone to talk to on a somewhat regular basis.

"Good Morning, Kai. Or should I say Good Afternoon? The morning is just about over." It had been years since I had any real attachments of any kind. It reminded me a bit of my Aunt Morgan. Adrian was nonchalant in his conversations with me, but I knew he enjoyed the company. He never asked any personal questions, and I was grateful for that.

"See you later, Adrian," I said, as I headed toward the walkway that led to the beach.

I wish I knew more about my family, or where I came from - but I don't. I never met my parents; my Aunt raised me. We lived in a village outside of Palmetto, Florida. We were in the swamp lands, and not far from the ocean. My Aunt used to say it was the best of both worlds in nature. She was always very vague, and never talked about my parents. Anytime I asked her she would just quickly look away and say, "I'd rather not." That's all she would say, then she would be off, and back to doing whatever she was doing before I had interrupted her. It kept her happy, and I was grateful to have someone to look after me. It was an unspoken agreement of sorts between the two of us. We had no other family that I knew of. She often took calls, and by the time I was a teenager she started leaving me alone when she went on her monthly trips; she was a very discreet woman. She made sure I had what I needed, and was in and out often. Once a month she would leave for a few days. I never really minded much. I was used to the solitude and quite enjoyed it.

My imagination would always keep me entertained for hours. Sometimes I would pretend that I was with my parents; they were always young and beautiful. I'd imagine the three of us waking up early, and having breakfast together before we went out to explore the marshes, or look for unique shells and rocks on the shore. They were so in love, and always laughing. The three of us would hold hands, and tease one another lovingly. They loved me more than anything, and we explored the world together. Sometimes I thought about my parents, and sometimes I didn't. Other times I would just wonder what could have happened that would have forced them into a position to give up their child. I'd ask myself what could be so impossible to make you walk away from the very life you brought into this world? Then I would wonder how they could have just gone on with their lives always knowing that I was out there, but never coming back for me. Then I'd start hating them, so I'd stop thinking about them entirely. I had become very familiar with emotional self-preservation at a very early age. It was around the same time I finally realized that no one was ever coming back for me - I had no parents. Eventually Mother's Day, and Father's Day became just ordinary days for me. When other children in school were making crafts and cards for their parents the art teacher would find another little project for me to do - always with eyes full of pity. I finally stopped expecting a card or a phone call on birthdays, and I even stopped imagining our reunion, and the multitude of things I'd catch them up on about my life.

I'd find other ways to entertain myself while my Aunt was

away. I would walk along the shore, hike alongside the lagoons looking for gators and wildlife, and I'd photograph for hours and hours. I'd photograph everything that caught my attention. I always had a fascination with preserving memories and moments just as I saw them at that very instant. I felt so connected to nature, and so drawn to the water. It was the only time I didn't mind the quiet sadness that was always there tugging at my heart. When my Aunt would return from her trips she would look even more beautiful than usual, well rested, and in great spirits. She was beautiful. I couldn't quite put my finger on her age and she would just laugh whenever I'd ask her. My Aunt Morgan was about my height, with rich chocolate colored hair, and dark green eyes. She had a beautiful figure, and the same fair complexion as I did. There was no mistaking that we were related. I'd ask her about her time away, and she would just squint her eyes a bit, smile, and say, "It's always amazing, Kai. One day I am going to tell you all about it, then take you with me," and finally the day came that she did - it was on my eighteenth birthday, when we come of age.

The most significant thing I remember about that night was how easily I accepted this impossible thing she was telling me. My complete lack of surprise was almost more alarming than finding out that I was actually part mythical sea creature. It all made perfect sense, the fact that she would leave once a month, always looked beautiful, never aging, and never really having a man in her life. It was also in that moment that I realized how much she had given up raising me all of these years. She could have stayed in the water, or hunted. She did neither of those things because she wouldn't risk exposure, and didn't want to move me from town to town. She explained that she would go to the water as it called her during the full moon cycles, and fought the urge to hunt. In many ways, I feel like I was born that night - or at least that it was the most important night of my life.

Aunt Morgan walked me to the water's edge and explained everything in her sweet voice. "Everyone handles themselves differently, Kai. It is going to take time to adjust and to learn to control your urges and cravings," she explained. I didn't understand any of what she meant that night; I only truly heard about half of what she told me. I'd later learn more, and I'd later truly appreciate all that she tried to warn me of that night. She took my hand and guided me into the water with her. Once we were shoulder deep, she looked at me and said, "Close your eyes, and go under. I'll be near, but tonight is yours to discover yourself." I did as she instructed. I hesitated before going under the water. I was suddenly confused. I grimaced, shook my head, and ran my hands frantically through my hair, "Every full moon?" I asked. "Is it just for one night?

So what are we, weremermaids?" I could not believe that word actually just escaped my lips. Aunt Morgan was nodding her head as I asked her this, as if she expected the confusion.

"It's more than simply one night, Kai. It is the lunar cycle beginning with the waxing gibbous to the change of a full moon, and then back to a waning gibbous when the moon fades back to about ninety five percent illumination, is when it's over. The time between these phases of waxing gibbous to waning gibbous is always slightly different, but it's about four days total. You will feel it - it becomes very natural and instinctive." She ran her hand through my hair, looked at me with compassionate eyes, and sighed. "I'm so sorry, Kai. I hate this for you. It's just who we are, it's in our blood. Our blood line was cursed by the old ones long ago - so that we would suffer as women not truly belonging to one world or the other, and never holding on to true love. There was a time when our kind lived only in the water. There were no such things as hybrids, so to speak."

I interrupted her, "And my mother, my father? What are they?" I said practically choking on my impossible words.

"Your mother is no longer a hybrid. She sacrificed all of her light to the old ones to save your father who is human. He knows nothing of you, Kai. She fell in love with him, but knew she could never truly be with him. The temptation to seek him out was much too painful and powerful. Her hunger for blood was one of the strongest I've ever known; she understood that she could not guarantee she would never hurt him, so she let her will, light, and freedom be taken. She is servant to the sea now and has very dark magic. There is almost nothing left of the being she once was - she is extremely dangerous." Aunt Morgan paused for a moment, looked off towards the moon, then lowered her eyes to the water. "She is a monster now, Kai."

I was sobbing now, my shoulders were shaking back and forth, my chest was heaving, and if I could have torn myself from the inside of my own body and escaped I would have. "I can't," I cried. "I can't hear anymore!" And with that I dove into the ocean. I swam faster and harder than I ever had, hoping the waves would take me under, and out of this nightmare of a night into dark silence. I wanted to die. I prayed for it, but I didn't. The moment I descended under the water I felt myself changing. I felt electricity shoot through my blood, I was more aware of every part of myself, I could hear the ocean in a way that I could not have imagined two minutes before, and I was breathing underwater! I could smell all of the different molecules under the water - I could feel all of life I was surrounded by, and see all of the beauty. I felt my hair brush against my shoulders, then flow back behind again like a long dark cape. It felt like weightless strands of silk. I tasted the salt, but not the way I did before this night when I'd accidentally swallow a mouthful in the ocean. It was much more natural, and didn't burn my throat or leave me feeling dehydrated. "This is really happening," I whispered. I could feel my body transforming into something else - I felt my waist tighten, and a tingling sensation across my thighs that worked its way down my legs, over my knees, all the way to each toe one by one. It felt like a thousand tiny electric surges bouncing, and swimming through my blood beginning at my waist and working their way to my feet. My legs effortlessly molded into a magnificent tail that was at least 5 feet long. There was no pain at all. I ran my hands along my tail, and felt the smoothness and its strength - my strength. I was so strong! I could see perfectly, and somehow, I was able to understand what the sea life was feeling as well. At first the sights and sounds were overwhelming, it was all almost too loud and too bright, but I adjusted. The colors were almost neon, the vibrancy was something I'd only ever seen a hint of in artwork; there were no colors here that I'd ever come close to seeing in the natural world on land. I swam all night that night. I had turned into my true self.

After a few months, the craving to hunt and kill began taking over - haunting me. It took me a very long time to come to terms with what I was. I had a very difficult time in the beginning. I started making one wrong decision after another. Aunt Morgan always gave me privacy and distance, but I knew she didn't approve of the decisions I was making and how I was living my life. She never outright judged me, and seemed to understand that I needed to feed my demons. She always seemed to quietly understand the sadness that I lived with. It haunted me. I think she always sort of got that. I never wanted her to know just how dark things had gotten for me. I moved out right after high school. Before I knew it, years of one toxic relationship after another, wild nights, and self-destructive behavior just passed me by, and we had lost touch completely. My Aunt Morgan and I hadn't spoken in years. I knew that she was powerful enough to sense me, but I also knew I was not ready to face her. It had been a very long time since I was close with anyone. It seemed that anyone I ever tried to get close to ended up badly hurt, or worse. That was not a path I was eager, or willing to revisit anytime soon. I suddenly realized that this year's birthday would be spent alone, just as the last several birthdays were spent and that was just what I needed.

I forced my thoughts back to the here and now. I walked along the beach, and watched the beautiful black horses running freely over the sand. I was jealous of them. They looked so wild and free without any restrictions or internal struggles. Then again, they were not mermaids with a hunger and thirst for blood either. I was only a couple of days away from the next full moon cycle - which meant my light was already beginning to separate from my body. I decided I would spend the next day looking for someone to play with. I didn't hunt last month; I swam for the entire cycle. I was starting to feel the hunger and the thirst again. The moon was nearly full. I had a day at best to choose my next victim.

About a mile west of where the horses were running, I could see a group of guys, and a few girls not far from where I was standing. There were several tourists on the island this week, which made things even easier. They were throwing a Frisbee around. Some of the guys were surfing, and a few of the girls were lounging on the beach doing their best to age themselves with all the sun damage they could soak up in one day. One might venture to assume that it was humans that thought they would stay young and beautiful forever for as much damage as they did to themselves. "Carelessness," I whispered to myself. I walked along past them casually. I could feel the young men's eyes all focus on me, and follow me as I walked along. I could hear the girls huffing their disapproval and practically feel their eyes rolling at the men's not so subtle interest in me. I was almost ready to laugh to myself when I was thrown off balance by a sand covered figure suddenly at my feet that rode in with one of the more impressive waves; I nearly fell to the ground. Of course, I didn't fall, I had amazing reflexes, but I was a bit annoyed.

"Wow, that was pretty embarrassing," he said.

"No worries. We both survived the collision," I replied smugly, brushing the sand from my legs. He brushed himself off as well as he stood up. He was nearly six feet tall, with very short light brown hair, deep brown eyes, an olive complexion, and perfect teeth. He was muscular, but lean - not bulky.

"I'm Kevin, and I really am sorry about the collision," he flashed a brilliant smile.

"I'm Kai. Honestly, no worries." I started walking away.

"Hey, wait. Can I at least try to make this up to you? I'm never going to live this down to my buddies, if they see me have the opportunity to meet a girl as beautiful as you are and completely fail." I looked up at him and smiled. You are just the guy I am looking for, I thought to myself.

"Sure, let's go grab a drink," I replied.

"Now?"

"Now," I replied.

"Awesome. Give me like two minutes to grab my stuff." He ran towards the others, gave one of his male companions a high five, and was back by my side all within the window of about forty five seconds. As we started walking off the beach back towards town, I couldn't help but notice the guys all making animated gestures to one another while laughing, and slapping each other's hands as if they had just realized the horse they bet on in a race had won something for them. Out of the corner of my eye I also noticed one small dark haired girl looking our way hastily, throwing her black knit cover up over her red bikini with tears in her eyes. She was obviously hurt by his complete lack of attention and affection for her. Boys will be boys, I thought. I hated that expression.

We walked along for a bit in silence. I was bored to tears. Finally, he broke the silence long enough to complement me on my dress. He drank me in with his eyes and said, "You look so great in that dress." It was a short, white, cotton, sleeveless dress that had tiny cherries all throughout the pattern. The neckline was low and square which showed off my bust, and the back was cut out very low. It fitted just snug enough to be sexy, but not sloppy. I was growing tired of him gawking so I initiated conversation again.

"How long are you on the island for?" I decided I might as well spend the afternoon with the guy and get to know him a little.

"We head home in three days. There is a pretty big party going on tonight, and then we are headed out to do a little drinking Saturday night too. You should come," he said.

I didn't turn until tomorrow night, and if I planned on spending the afternoon with him today, I certainly did not want to waste my entire evening with him as well.

"I actually can't tonight, but I can meet up with you tomorrow night if that works."

"That definitely works."

"Let's stop here," I said, and pointed to the Island Gator. It was a small bar on the island that overlooked one of the lagoons. It was nothing fancy, but I liked it. There were almost never any locals here. It was a bar that catered to tourists and out of towners. The inside was decorated to look like the inside of a big swamp boat with alligator decor on almost everything, they had drinks called gator juice, and even put little brown and green plastic alligators in your drinks. There was outdoor seating as well in their screened in patio area overlooking the lagoon. From every seat outside you had an incredible view of moss draped cypress trees, and an abundance of wildlife that make their home in the swampland areas of the island. Tourists loved it here. I couldn't disagree with the appreciation either, it was a unique little spot.

We sat at the end of the bar away from the other patrons. The bartender made his way over after a few minutes looking less than enthused to be on the side of the bar that was serving instead of enjoying. "What can I get for you?" he asked.

"I'll just have a beer, whatever is on tap is fine," said Kevin.

"And for you, your usual?"

"Thanks, Terry. That would be awesome," I knew Terry from coming in from time to time. He always remembered your drink, and minded his own business. These were both amazing qualities in any bartender.

"Yep," he said, as he served Kevin his beer and placed my gin and tonic with extra lime in front of me. Terry grabbed Kevin's money from the bar, made change for him, and went back to his other patrons. Terry was about thirty, with bleach blonde messy hair that fell over his eyes, sleeves of tattoos on both arms, and a little bit of a beer belly.

"He seems happy to be here," Kevin said sarcastically while gesturing towards Terry.

"He's not so bad," I said. "Bartenders in destination areas have to endure an entirely different kind of clientele than bartenders in regular areas. He is probably just mentally preparing himself for the weekend here," I laughed.

"I guess so. My boys and I get pretty rowdy, and have a good time with the ladies anytime we are away," he bragged.

"Who were the girls with you guys?"

He shifted a little in his bar stool, and took a sip of his beer.

He smacked his lips together, and made a sound that indicated he enjoyed what he was drinking. "They are just girls from back home. One is my buddy's girlfriend, the other two are just girls we are friends with that come along when we go away," he explained.

"It seemed like the little brunette looked a little disappointed that you were leaving her behind today. Is there a story there?" I asked.

"No story really. We are friends, and she may like me a little more than I like her. It happens, and sometimes other things happen when friends get together and have a good time. I think it means more to her. It's not really my problem, right?"

"I guess not," I replied. Any hesitation I may have had about seeing him the following night completely dissipated. The small part of my soul that tries clinging on to me before it all but disappears during the cycle, tempted me to consider ending our time together here and just swimming again this month - not a chance now.

"Kai is a unique name. Do you have a last name, Kai?" he asked.

"Kai Cordula, but you can just call me Kai."

"Can I just call you beautiful?" He flashed me that perfect smile again. I literally had to bite my tongue to stop myself from telling him how completely ridiculous he sounded. I couldn't believe that human girls fell for guys like this over and over.

"How about we begin with Kai, and see how it goes," I was smiling at him now with my eyes.

"How old are you, what do you do, where are you from? I want to know everything about you," He said in between giant gulps of his beer.

I sipped my gin and tonic, and twirled strands of my hair with my index finger. I was getting a bit restless.

"I will be twenty-five in about a month, right now I am taking a break from real life, and I'm from a little bit of everywhere. I'd hate to ruin the mystery for you, so I guess you're going to have to work with vague," I teased.

"Fair enough," he said. We spent another couple of drinks discussing meaningless details. He told me what types of music he liked, bragged about all his athletic accomplishments in college, and talked about himself like he was trying to sell something to me. He insulted others for humor, and told me stories about guys he and his buddies tortured in high school and college simply because they could. I was liking him less and less with every poorly structured sentence that escaped his lips. He was actually quite mean. He talked about other human beings as if they were beneath him, and totally irrelevant. He was already feeling the effects of his beer, and his words were getting sloppy. He didn't bother asking me anything more about myself, which I was grateful for - I knew it was getting close to time for him to suit up for his party tonight, and whatever lady was lucky enough to be his arm candy and trophy this evening. I finished my drink, gathered my keys and bag I had sitting on the bar in front of me, and put my hand on his thigh.

"I have to get going." I stood up, brushed my hair back behind my shoulders to give him an unobstructed view of my cleavage, and shifted my weight from side to side slowly to draw his eyes back down to my stomach and hips.

"You're all mine tomorrow night, okay?" I said in a soft seductive voice.

He put his hands around my waist and pulled me in to him so our faces were just inches apart.

"Hell yeah, I am. I'll meet you here at eight, gorgeous."

I bit my lower lip, then pulled from his embrace. "Be good tonight, Kevin." I looked back over my shoulder as I walked out of the bar and he smiled at me as he settled the tab. I had a feeling it would only be a matter of minutes before my empty seat next to him was taken by one of the girls on the other side of the bar that had been looking his way for the past hour and a half, and I was perfectly okay with that.

The next morning, I woke up feeling wired and anxious. I knew it was only a matter of hours before the full moon, but the anticipation and hunger I was experiencing was overwhelming. All I could hear in my mind were the noises of crashing waves, rain, lightning striking, and melodic laughter. I couldn't quiet my head at all this morning. The voices telling me to swim, to hunt, to kill were deafening. I thought I might scream. I showered, dressed, and began making my way out of the hotel for a run. I passed Robert and Rebecca Claude in the hall purposely not making eye contact and looking rushed. They didn't seem to think much of it one way or the other. I was so on edge, I had to get out into the air and closer to the water. I was beginning to feel claustrophobic in the hotel - even though it was enormous. It felt like the walls were slowly narrowing in on me inch by inch. I made my way quickly through the beautiful lobby to the large doors when I heard some-one calling my name.

"Hey, Kai. Hang on," cried Molly in almost a shout. Molly and I had become friendly since the night she checked me in here when I arrived. She was my age, extremely kind, and we would occasionally chit chat here and there on my way in or out.

"Molly, I'm sorry. I am in sort of a hurry," I said.

"I see that. I was just wondering if you wanted to get together sometime this week. I see you with your camera around your neck sometimes, and was wondering if you wanted to go for a hike or something sometime and get some shots out there. I know all the best trails on the island."

"I didn't realize you photographed," I said.

"I do. Probably not that well, but it's been a hobby of mine for a while." She looked down. "I know you're busy, I shouldn't have stopped you. I'm sorry."

"No worries, Molly. Let me get back to you on it okay?" I shot her a genuine smile.

"Absolutely," she said. She seemed satisfied with that for now. I actually liked Molly a lot and it had been years since I had a real girlfriend. Maybe I would take her up on that offer, but I wasn't really in the mood to become best friends with anyone today, so it would have to wait. I passed Adrian on the way to the beach, and gave a quick wave as I began jogging.

The smell of the salt in the air immediately began to soothe me. I felt more relaxed as I ran along the ocean. The voices in my head were beginning to quiet a bit, and the sounds I was focused on were the ones of the nature and space around me. Before the full moon, I always felt a kind of buzz come over me. I felt wilder, and more subject to my basic needs. I ran for a couple of miles, before turning back towards the hotel again. The wind on my face and in my hair felt amazing. I thought about tonight, and I thought about Kevin. I hadn't hunted last month, and the month before that I simply took a random guy I spotted on the beach trying to date rape some girl that could barely stand from all she drank that night, let alone free herself from his disgusting restraint on her. I hadn't planned on killing anyone so soon after my arrival to the island, but I couldn't swim by and allow that to happen. It was a kill, but there was little satisfaction from it. It was over in seconds. I came out of the water in nothing but glistening beads of water rolling down my body. That got his attention quickly. I used magic on the girl to manipulate her into walking back to where she came from with no memory of her night on the beach. As she walked away I devoured him, then took him under with me. It was all over so suddenly, it was almost as if it hadn't happened at all. It had been months since I hunted my prey and played the game of cat and mouse I loved to play so much. As I ran I thought of nothing else but preparing for tonight.

On my way back to the Cliffside I stopped in the one little shop on the island I hadn't explored yet. It was a quaint little used book store called Sea Side Stories. I had walked past here almost every day and mentally noted how much I enjoyed the name of the small shop each time, but I never stopped in. I loved used book stores and libraries. This one had a certain charm about it that I found myself drawn to. It was a one story red brick building covered in green vines, and moss. There was one large picture window to the right, and a simple white door on the left. There were books displayed on a table on the other side of the window, and a small sign on the door that simply said, welcome. The sign was wooden with a painted scene of the sun setting over the cliffs alongside the ocean.

There was a bell attached to the door that rang when the door opened to let the owner know he had a customer. The bell chimed, and a man standing on a step ladder straightening books on a high shelf looked my way. Without smiling he simply said, "Good Afternoon. Let us know if you have any questions." I looked around but didn't see anyone other than him in the shop, which made me wonder who "us" in fact was. He noticed me looking around.

"It's just a figure of speech, Miss. I'm not a crazy shop keeper keeping company with imaginary acquaintances here…at least not just yet," He finally smiled. I smiled back at him,

"Well that's good to know. Thank you."

He climbed down from his ladder, and walked toward me.

"My name is Jeremy. This is my shop. Let me know if I can help you find anything." He had a smooth and soft tone to his voice. He had an accent that I could not quite place. It was a cross between a New England accent, and Canadian. I guessed he was in his early forties. He had short chestnut brown hair that he kept just a little longer in front, bright hazel eyes, high cheek bones, a strong jaw bone, and perfectly symmetrical features. He was a very good looking guy. He was thin, and stood a little over six feet tall. I shifted my weight from side to side, and realized I was wrapping my fingers around one another a bit nervously.

"Thank you. My name is Kai. I'm staying at the Cliffside - for a few months now. This is one of the only places on the island I haven't visited yet," I said. Why was I telling this guy so much about myself? I wondered.

"Well, welcome to Gray Mist and enjoy." I smiled, and began exploring the store. The aisles were narrow, and the book shelves nearly reached the ceiling. He had just about everything you could imagine. I grabbed a random book off the shelf and opened it without even looking at the title. I loved the smell of an old book, there is nothing like it in the world, I thought. I flipped through the pages and realized I had a book on photography in my hand. I walked around the little shop with the same book in my hand and noticed that there was another room set up the same way towards the back. I walked on the oversized thick oriental style rug that covered the hardwood floors wondering why anyone would cover such beautiful floors. The back room had tons of books on mythology, folklore, fantasy, and ancient cultures. There were two small round wicker tables with two sets of wicker chairs for people to sit, and read back here. I always thought it would be great to own my own little book shop one day - that is if I were an actual human with a normal existence. I sat and read for a while before getting back up to return the book to the shelf I found it on. I thanked Jeremy on my way back towards the front of the store. "I will be back to buy that book," I promised, "I was just out for a run and I don't have any cash on me."

He nodded. "Very good. Have an enjoyable day, and we hope to see you again soon."

"Thanks, you too," I said on my way out the door. I could have stayed in there all day and night, but I had a date to get ready for.

CHAPTER
Three

THE REST OF THE AFTERNOON seemed to move in slow motion. It seemed like an eternity, but the time finally came to begin getting ready for my evening with Kevin. I decided to wear my dark blue, silk, backless dress. It had a high neck, a completely open back, and hit right above my knee. It was very sexy. The only jewelry I wore was a black string necklace with a single pearl strung through it. I wore very little makeup, just a touch of a light bronzer to highlight my high cheek bones, black mascara, and a soft pink lip gloss. I piled my long hair on top of my head in a loose, yet sexy bun. I took one last look in the full-length mirror and was satisfied with the image looking back at me. I slipped on a pair of black strappy sandals, and I was off to meet him. It was already almost eight, but it wouldn't take very long to walk to the Island Gator.

I enjoyed the quiet on my way to meet Kevin. All I could hear was the ocean in the distance and the sound of my heels clicking on the pavement as I walked on. The air was warm and still. The light of the full moon was glorious. Everything about the scenery around me was romantic. The connection that I felt to the water and the moon had replaced any connection I would otherwise feel to my soul. That is simply the nature of what happens to my kind during the full moon, we lose our souls entirely. The first few times it happened to me I was confused, and it was difficult to process how I felt about not having a soul. Eventually you get used to it, and ultimately you give in to it. There is nothing else like it; there is no pain, no remorse, and no conscience. There is a freedom that comes with not having a moral responsibility to the things you have done. Our souls return once the cycle is over, but we are not as closely attached to them as humans are. The longer we go on, the less we can feel our souls. Every once in a while, I can feel my soul trying to cling to me once the full moon is over. I've learned to almost turn it off. We must. Otherwise, we would go raving mad from all the emotional and mental burdens that having a soul brings to one's life. That is why these past few months have been so confusing for me. Something felt different. Why was I suddenly thinking so much about my victims? That was the entire reason I left my previous home. I was seeing their blood everywhere I stepped foot. I was turning immortal in about a month, maybe that had something to do with all of this.

Without even realizing how far I had walked I was suddenly in front of the bar. I straightened my dress out, pulled my shoulders back slightly, and walked in. Kevin was sitting in the same place we were the other day when we had a couple of afternoon drinks together here. He had a bottle of beer in one hand and the other was resting on the very attractive red head he was chatting up that was sitting next to him.

"Classic," I said aloud. I let him enjoy her company for a moment before I interrupted. The jukebox was playing reggae, and the dimly lit bar was full. I walked over to an open spot at the bar next to a good-looking guy looking down at his drink.

"Excuse me," I said, "I just want to get in and grab a drink." He glanced quickly at me then looked away.

"Go right ahead," he said without looking at me again. I was a little intrigued by his complete lack of interest in me. There was something else about him, something that made me want to know more. He had dark wavy hair that nearly touched his jawbone, big dark eyes that looked almost black with hints of green, fair skin, and full lips. He was more beautiful than handsome. He was thin; It was hard to tell because he was sitting down how tall he was, but I guessed he was about 5'10 or so. He wore khaki colored cargo pants with a white short sleeved button up shirt that had maroon pinstripes. I looked at him again and thought about saying something to him. Just as I started to open my mouth to speak, Terry was right in front of me with a hurried look on his face.

"What's it going to be tonight, Kai, your usual?"

"Yeah that's fine," I said trying to hide the irritation in my voice. He was already pouring my drink anyway. I saw Kevin from across the bar finally noticing me and waving me over. I smiled and put my finger up to indicate I'd be there in a moment. He smiled, whispered something in the redhead's ear, and she walked away from him. She caught my eye line for just a moment, and gave me a seductive smile. There was something familiar about the way she walked, but before I could think anymore about it she was gone.

"Keep the change, Terry," I said, and made my way towards Kevin.

"Hey beautiful," he stammered. He was already drunk.

"Hey there, yourself. How are you?" I asked.

"Outstanding," he boasted. "I missed you," he said.

"Did you?" I eyed him up suspiciously.

"I did. Would I lie to you?" He spun back and forth on his bar stool, and took another gulp of his beer. He ran his fingers through his hair, and finally took a moment to take me in with his eyes. "Wow," he said. "Get over here." He grabbed me by the waist, and pulled me in to kiss me. I gently pulled away.

"Hang on," I sat down in the bar stool that the red head had claimed as hers before I showed up. "I think I have some catching up to do."

He slapped both hands down on the bar, "Bartender, I think we are going to need some shots down here," he exclaimed. I laughed, and shook my head. As I looked up to see if Terry was making his way towards us, I caught the guy I almost talked to a few minutes ago looking at me. He darted his eyes in the other direction when I looked back at him. Over the next two hours I suffered through Kevin's ridiculous tales from the night before, three shots of tequila, and too many poorly chosen eighties rock songs on the juke box to count.

"Kai, Kai, Kai...I want to keep you." He was laughing at himself now. "Can I take you back home with me when we leave the island?"

"I'm sure you would get bored with me after a few days."

"Never. It would never happen. There is not a boring bone in your body. I can tell." He ran his hands along my thighs, and then grabbed my knee firmly. "So are you caught up enough to let me get you somewhere a little more one on one yet?" Now he had his cell phone in his hand. He was so obnoxious that he made no effort to try to hide what he was texting from me. He actually read out loud as he keyed the words into his phone, "This is lucky number 5 this week. She is going to get it good tonight," he laughed as he said it out loud. I stood up from my bar stool, finished the last sip of my drink, and looked into his hazed over eyes.

"Let's get out of here," I said in a voice that could only mean one thing...to him. On our way out I looked over where my mystery guy had been sitting. He was already gone. Kevin trailed behind me with both hands on my waist as to mark his territory as we walked out.

He was singing along with the jukebox now, "Oh oh, we're halfway there, oh oh living on a prayer."

As soon as we were outside of the bar he seemed to magically sober up quite a bit.

"Can I get you back to my place. My buddies will be there, but they are always up for a party too." He was actually serious. I hid my contempt for him, and that ridiculous idea well.

"I thought we could go to the beach, near the cliffs. No one is ever anywhere near there this time of night," I said. I leaned in to kiss him softly on the lips.

"That's an excellent idea. You're a smart girl," he slapped my backside, and we started walking. "I wish I could meet more girls as cool as you. I mean, sometimes fun is just fun. We are young and this is what life is all about right now," he rambled on. I just listened to him, or at least made an effort to pretend to listen to him. We were only steps away from the area on the beach we were headed for. We found a spot and sat down together. There was absolutely no one in sight. We passed a few people a few blocks before we hit the beach, but no one since. There were no lights on the beach, no sounds, except the waves crashing on the cliffs. There is no one here to hear your screams, I thought. I could practically taste his blood already. I wanted him right now. I wanted to lunge at him and take everything from him at that moment, but I controlled myself. I thought I'd take my time with this one.

"Get over here, girl." He grabbed me, and pulled me on top of him. He was laying on his back, and I was straddling him now. He had his hands on my thighs, then moved a hand behind my neck to pull me towards him. I let him kiss me. I was surprised that he actually wasn't too bad of a kisser. His lips were soft, and he gently sucked on my bottom lip at the end of each kiss. I could tell that he was used to being dominant with girls. He flipped me over so that he could lay on top of me. He pulled the pins out of my hair, and let it fall loosely around my shoulders. He started to pull my skirt up, but I stopped him.

"Not yet," I said. "I want to go in the water."

He smiled and stood up.

"You are a smart girl," he said and started tearing off his shirt, and pulling off his shorts. I sat up with my arms supporting my weight behind me, and my knees crossed watching him undress. "Like what you see?" he asked in a cocky voice flashing me that brilliant smile.

"Not bad," I teased. I stood up and kissed him again. Now we were really kissing. Our tongues found one another, and his hands had found their way under my dress and on to my bare skin. I felt my stomach tighten with an almost cramping sensation, and my hand was making its way towards the waist band of his boxers. My own heart was beating faster and faster. I pulled away from him, took a step back, and gently tugged on my dress at my shoulders. I let it fall down to my hips. Kevin stood there biting his lower lip. I wasn't wearing anything under my dress.

"Wow," he managed to say. I smiled. I gave my dress another slight tug at my hips, and let it fall to the sand. I carefully stepped out of it, ran my fingers through my hair, and ran towards the water.

"Come and get me, if you want me," I yelled. He ran out after me and grabbed me. His hands were all over everywhere he could reach in the matter of seconds. I was kissing him wildly. I wanted him now, I needed him now. I can't wait any longer, I thought. I was going mad with desire and hunger for him. I grabbed him by the back of his neck, started nibbling on his ear. He was moaning now. I licked his earlobe and kissed his neck while his hands explored my bare breasts. It was time, oh God was it time. My head snapped forward, and I sunk my teeth into his flesh. He was delicious. I felt his hands drop from my breasts, and his body tighten up with panic. He screamed.

"Mmm keep screaming, I love it," I moaned. I fed on him until I felt his heart slow down. He tasted amazing. I was shaking from pleasure and excitement. I pulled him under the water with me with one strong movement. My tail was now exposed, so I used it to wrap around him to keep a tight hold on him. It wrapped around him like a giant snake. He was gone. I didn't want to have to hold on to his body with my arms. The water was dark, and it was high tide. I needed to swim out a little further, and deeper with him. I passed a tiger shark as I went out further into the water that appreciated my kill. I expressed my recognition, and kept swimming. I could hear their thoughts, they didn't speak with words as humans do. Tiger sharks were known throughout the waters as creatures that would feed on anything. They had no fear, and could not be trusted - they would even scavenge on dead whales. I almost didn't see it, they are masters of disguise and can camouflage themselves very well when hunting. Sharks as a rule don't attack mermaids. In fact, in most cases they will protect us from harm, but it was always best practice to keep moving when encountering one - especially when no one else is around. I swam out another few feet, and let the ocean take him for me. A gift to the gods, I always thought.

"You're welcome," I said, and swam back towards the shore. I wasn't in the mood to spend the rest of the night swimming like I usually was after a kill. I thought I was satisfied, but now I felt a little restless…or something. I swam all the way back to the shore, looked around to make sure no one was in sight, and stepped back on to the sand. My dress was still laying there, as were his clothes, wallet, and cell phone. I put my dress back on and straightened myself out. I walked to the water's edge and threw his things in the ocean. The ocean would take care of it. If there is one thing to be said for sea life, it is that we take care of our own. Nothing ever surfaces that the water does not wish to surface. It's always been that way. That's one of the numerous reasons our existence will never really be proven.

I decided to walk a bit further to settle myself down. There was a spot I loved on the island alongside of the beach where a magnificent sixty-five-foot oak tree stood. I often stopped there to think, read, or just people watch. Contrary to the existence I lived, I was quite taken with humans. I love watching them; I did spend a good part of my life thinking I was one of them after all. I envied them and pitied them at the same time. I found this unique little spot on the island one afternoon by accident when I was out hiking and photographing. I had been kind of in love with it ever since. As I approached my spot from the beach I admired the magnificence of the grand branches of the tree in the distance. From tip to tip, the longest branch distance had to be close to one hundred and eighty-five feet or so. It was hauntingly beautiful in the light of the full moon with the ocean as it's backdrop in the distance. I heard rustling, and assumed it was coming from small animals moving around. No…there was someone there sitting on the grassy area that surrounded the tree. I almost turned around to not be bothered until I realized who it was. It was him. It was my mystery guy from the bar.

He was sitting alone and he looked like he had been crying. I don't know what it was about him, but something about this guy tugged at my heart - even with no soul. I was positively over-whelmed with curiosity and intrigue. I watched him for a few minutes. I was too far from him to notice or hear me. I on the other hand had heightened senses, so I could observe him effortlessly from where I stood. I wasn't sure if he was local or not; if he was, then he was off limits. You never killed locals, there was too much risk of exposure when the locals started turning up missing left and right. People never noticed when tourists came and went - not really anyway. I had just taken Kevin tonight, but I was feeling restless. Perhaps this is what I was supposed to be drawn to. "This certainly wouldn't be the first time I've had more than one in a night," I whispered to myself with a smile. He was sitting with his knees pulled to his chest and his arms resting on his knees. His hair was messy, and he still had the same clothes on from earlier. He was crying. I could feel his loneliness; I wanted to know him. I didn't have a choice, I had to get closer to him. I had no idea what I would do once I reached him, but I was going. I started walking towards him when I saw someone else out of the corner of my eye. Was she coming out of the water? I wondered. She was! It was that redhead from earlier tonight at the bar. No wonder there was something so familiar about the way she moved. She was heading towards him, and that could only mean one thing. "No!" I screamed in my head. I sprinted towards her, and was standing in front of her before I had time to think about what I would say or do once we were face to face

"Hello, Kai," she said. "Is this one yours, too?"

CHAPTER

SHE STOOD IN FRONT OF ME with an eyebrow arched, and an impatient look on her face. Her wavy red hair was just past her shoulders, and blowing in the breeze. She had bright green eyes, a perfectly structured small oval face, and full pink lips. She was about 5'7, with a gorgeous figure, and she smelled like water lilies. Her long red dress was blowing in the breeze as well.

She put her hands on her hips, "Well?" She asked. I was still questioning every second of what was happening here.

"Who are you? How do you know my name, and why are you here?" I said all at once.

She sighed heavily. "Do you typically answer questions with more questions?" She rolled her eyes. "Not a becoming quality in a lady, you know that right?" She started walking towards him again.

"Stop," I pleaded. "No, he is not mine, he may be local. Leave him be. There are dozens of other disposable ones on the island tonight."

She smiled. "I know. I've already had three."

"Three?" I grabbed her by the arm and started walking her in the opposite direction of my lonely mystery man. "Are you crazy?" You can't just show up, and start taking lives in excess like this! I live here." I was getting angry now, and she had yet to tell me who she was. "Who the hell are you, and how do you know my name?" I asked her slowly, purposely dragging my words out.

She sighed. "My name is Cleo, and everyone knows your name…you are Ava's daughter."

I shook my head in confusion. I wasn't sure I should even trust her.

"Ava?" I asked.

"Yes, Ava - and I don't think you are ready to know much more than that just yet."

The words were barely out of her mouth and she was already running towards the ocean. She dove into the water beautifully, leaving her dress behind as she turned. She flipped her shiny red tail in the air behind her, and disappeared into the dark blue waters. I admired how beautiful she was for a moment…only for a moment. I looked back to where my mystery man was. I was further away from him now than I was before, but I could see that he remained there unharmed. It was my turn to cry now, only I couldn't. I walked closer to the ocean and sat there until nearly sunrise trying to metabolize what happened in the hours before. I could feel my light returning, and now it really was my turn to cry.

The next few days were sort of a blur. I didn't leave my room most of that week. I must have been in some type of a shock. I'd lay on my king-sized bed staring up at the white ceiling for hours. I'd lay there on my back, slowly rubbing my bare feet against one another atop of the cool pearl colored silk sheets beneath me, while I twirled long strands of hair with my index finger. I imagined I was in a beautiful garden sitting on a metal wired fence. On one side of the fence there was a sign that read "Angry", and on the other side of the fence there was a sign that read "Devastated" - I was sitting on the fence between the two trying to decide which side of that fence I would land on when I fell. There were red roses on one side, and white roses on the other. "How could this be happening?" I said. I had no idea how many others were here, how long they were staying, or what anyone wanted from me. Why does my mother suddenly have an interest in me? I remembered Aunt Morgan's thoughtful expression, and the coolness of the tone of her voice when she said, "She is a monster now, Kai." I knew at that moment how much she believed her words and how much I believed them too. I sat up quickly. I knew what was happening.

"My birthday." I said aloud. "My immortality, that's why the sudden interest in me. That has to be it." That was it. My birthday was approaching, along with my gift of immortally. It was only a few weeks away. I wish I had paid more attention to Aunt Morgan when I was younger. She tried giving me lessons, and passing knowledge on to me that explained all of this. I never cared to know. I think there was a part of me that didn't think I'd make it to see my twenty-fifth birthday. Was I ever so mistaken, and now I was certain that I was in the center of something that I couldn't begin to understand.

There was a knock at the door, I thought about ignoring it and then heard, "Kai. I'm very sorry to disturb you, but I've not seen you out and about in a few days," there was a pause, then more knocking. She clearly was not going to go away. Rather than continue to ignore her, I opened the door.

I took a deep breath and flashed a tight smile at her.

"I'm fine, Molly. Thank you for checking in on me."

She smiled and nervously moved her keys from one hand to the other.

"Oh good," she said. "Adrian was asking about you yesterday morning when it occurred to me that no one has really seen you in days." She fidgeted around with the buttons on her blouse. Her dark blue eyes were honest and full of concern. "I'm sorry to have bothered you." She turned around to go.

I gently put my hand on her arm.

"It's fine, Molly - really. I've just been feeling a little under the weather." She opened her eyes wide and nodded her head as if everything made perfect sense to her now.

"Can I have something brought to you?"

"That won't be necessary. I'm feeling much better, thank you," I smiled.

"Okay then. If there is anything you need, please let us know. I am off in a few hours, but Mr. Edwards will be here this evening, and well...you know everyone," she said. Mr. Edwards was the hotel manager. He was an extremely kind man in his late fifties, and gave me plenty of privacy. I wanted to keep it that way. I exchanged polite greetings with the entire staff at the hotel, but Molly was the only one I really interacted with on a somewhat regular basis. I liked her.

"Got it. Thanks, Molly." She seemed satisfied with that. She smiled once more before turning to walk back down the long hallway. I was grateful she didn't ask me anything more or attempt to make any plans with me. I felt slightly guilty that I kept finding reasons not to spend time with her. She was such a nice girl, and I got the feeling that she didn't have many friends.

It couldn't have been more than a minute after I closed the door there was another knock.

"Molly, I'm fine," I said as I opened the door again.

"I'm happy to hear you are well, but I told you my name is Cleo." Cleo stood there with a tight smirk on her face, and one hand on her hip. Her long red hair was in a perfectly sculpted fish tail braid pulled to the right side of her face.

"What are you doing here? What the hell do you want with

me?" Every bit of my body was telling me not to trust this girl, but at the same exact time I couldn't help but want to know at least a little more about her. The only other mermaid I'd ever known was my Aunt Morgan. I knew they were out there. Of course, I heard the stories from other creatures under the sea - but I'd never met another like me. She walked in, and jumped on the bed. She laid on her stomach, and kicked her feet up behind her.

"You really do ask too many questions," she said laughing. "I'm not here to hurt you, Kai." I looked down at her sharply, "As if you could," I darted at her.

"Sassy. I like you more already." We simply looked at one another for a few moments. Maybe she was just as interested in me, as I was in her, I thought to myself. She broke the spell of silence at that moment.

"I'm not that interested in you, yes I can read your thoughts, and I've come to take you back where you belong."

Now it was my turn to sit down.

"Why would I go anywhere with you?"

"Why wouldn't you?" "What are you afraid of? I've been watching you for some time, and I know that you are very careful not to make any real connections with humans - it's not as if you have anything keeping you anywhere." She was not wrong. "Look, Ava is ready for you. It's as simple as that."

Suddenly I was overwhelmed with anger. I could feel the aggression surging through my body all the way to my fingertips that were tingling.

"I don't owe Ava anything. She abandoned me. She never came for me once I turned. I no longer have a relationship with my Aunt Morgan, and I couldn't even tell you if my father is dead or alive. The way I see it, I don't belong in the water any more or any less than I belong on land."

She waited a few seconds to make sure I was finished.

"Kai, you don't belong here at all. We are not like them. We are hunters. We hunt, we kill, and then we swim. You know all of this. Your little speech was super, cute but it's time for real talk." It was then that I realized what I must have known for quite some time.

"I don't want to hunt anymore. I don't want to kill anymore. Something inside me is changing. I can feel it. I don't enjoy the kill the way I once did. I have nightmares about my victims. I'm haunted by the sounds of their cries. I feel the pain I've caused. I don't want to do it again. I won't."

"Your behavior last night might indicate otherwise," she smirked. Then Cleo looked at me thoughtfully for a moment. Now I could hear her thoughts too. She was remembering what it felt like to have those feelings. She remembered how quickly she turned them off, and gave in to her true self. "You're wrong, Kai." She lifted herself off the bed, and walked towards the door. "You're wrong, and I'm not leaving this island without you." She let herself out, and closed the door quietly behind her after giving me one final hard look with those big bright eyes of hers.

"Well isn't this just lovely," I said aloud. What was I going to do with a mermaid following me around, and noting my every move? When I told her that I wanted nothing to do with Ava, I meant it. I'd never become her. I realized then that I had become her, and it needed to end now. I knew that I could turn without killing. I could swim. It was possible. It was completely possible. Suddenly it occurred to me that I was a little surprised that I was never curious about others like me. I never went around trying to seek them out or anything. I suppose I had just learned to live on my own. I was emotionally exhausted. I decided I'd go look for Cleo. She couldn't be very far, and she was most likely scouting the area for what would be her next prey anyway. I got showered, threw on a black tank top, and a long brown skirt, and hurried out. I pulled my hair back as I was walking out the door. I made my way through the hotel, and for once it seemed empty. I was able to make my way throughout the lobby, and out of the front doors without one interruption. As soon as I got outside I saw my mystery guy speaking to Adrian. They were laughing, and genuinely enjoying one another's company. I could sense that.

"Hey Kai. We were worried you skipped town on us without saying goodbye," said Adrian.

"Hey, Adrian. I wouldn't dream of it," I smiled.

My mystery guy was looking at me curiously. "Lee, this is Kai. Kai this is Lee." We shook hands.

"I've seen you around. It's nice to officially meet you," he said casually.

"It's nice to officially meet you as well." He smiled softly, then explained to Adrian that he was off to run errands. I watched him walk away, and probably let my stare linger a little longer than I should have. There was something about him that I was so drawn to. It was as if I could feel his vulnerability and pain. Adrian brought me back to reality.

"He is a sweet kid."

"How old is he," I asked.

"Lee is twenty-eight. He showed up on the island a few years ago alone - like you. He stayed on doing odd jobs here and there, and never left. Now he runs his own business here on the island. He runs nature and water tours. The tourists can't get enough of it, and he constantly refers his tourists to the restaurants, bars, and shops on the island which is part of the reason the locals love him so much too."

"So, he doesn't have any family on the island?"

"No - it's just him." I wondered what his story was, then I

wondered why I was so curious.

"Well have a good day, Adrian." I smiled, and started walking towards the book store I stumbled upon the other day.

I stopped in front of Sea Side Stories, and thought about how much I loved the name of this little store. The bell chimed as I entered. Jeremy was there once again straightening books on a shelf.

"She is a girl of her word," he said.

"I am. Or at least I try to be," I smiled at him.

"Come on in, and have another look. Let me know if you need anything."

"Thank you," I said. I entered the store and started going through the sections again one by one. I knew there was something I was looking for, and I'd know it when I would finally find it. I truly did love the smell of this store. Many of the books were old, and smelled of history and memories. I wondered how many hands some of these remarkable stories had passed through? How many people fell in love reading these books, became scholars, or lived in fantasy worlds for a brief period while they were swept away in these beautifully written words? It was beautiful. I envied humanity. I missed the time in my life when I thought I was nothing more than human. I was going to grow up, fall in love, have a family, and eventually leave this world. There were a few years that I was intoxicated by my life as a mermaid. I thought I was mad with happiness. I realize now, that I was simply mad. I was living a life of destruction, pain, and sorrow. I did terrible things. Things I can never make right again. I must live with that for eternity. Without realizing I had even picked it up, I had a book of underwater illustrations in my hands. I turned through the pages, and I saw a mermaid. She was glorious - and surprisingly accurately illustrated. I wondered how many men lived to tell the tales of the beautiful girls with tails in the sea. Clearly, there were several throughout history. The story of the mermaid was hardly anything new. Our existence would never be proven. I was certain of that. I was looking at this mermaid when the voice I heard startled me so much I nearly dropped the book.

"Hey Kai," she said sweetly. She grabbed the book from me and smiled. "Very nice," she said. She was dressed differently, but still had her long red wavy hair in a fishtail braid. She had on shiny peach lip gloss that lit her entire face up. She truly was breathtaking.

I gently took the book back from her.

"I was actually looking for you. Let's walk." I said goodbye to Jeremy. He didn't seem to notice, he was far too involved in whatever book he was reading. Cleo and I left the shop, and started walking towards the Island Gator. We found a spot near the back, and both ordered water.

"I want you to leave," I said quietly.

"I know," she replied. "I'd like to leave as well, but if I do not return with you I can't return." Suddenly I felt her fear. I could hear my Aunt Morgan's words again in my head, "She is a monster, Kai."

"Are you afraid of my mother?'

"Yes, and you should be as well. She is one of the most powerful creatures in the sea. Once you join her at her side, they say she will be just as powerful as the old ones."

"Okay, I will follow you. I feel like I need to meet her, but I am not staying." I could hear her thoughts telling me that it had to be my choice to stay anyway. "Then we will go - tonight," I said. We agreed to meet near the water not far from the giant oak tree after sunset. I made her promise not to hurt anyone on this island between now and then. She agreed, and then she left.

I wasn't sure how much time had passed as I sat in the back

corner of the bar alone lost in my thoughts. My thoughts and emotions were like giant tides crashing against the inside of my skull. With every crash, I saw images of so many things. I saw the people that I hurt, I saw the sea, I saw images of myself growing up, my Aunt Morgan, and flashes of red and black over and over. I remembered feelings of joy, sorrow, remorse, passion, anger, and emptiness all at once. I was swimming through waters of memories in my mind whether I liked it or not. The sound of the glass being set down on the table in front of me snapped me out of it.

"I just keep bumping into you," he said in a soft voice. I looked up at Lee, and immediately felt my entire body relax. I smiled, then nodded at the chair across from me gesturing him to sit down.

"It's a small island," I said.

"That it is," he said as he sat down across from me. I smiled. There was something about Lee that I was positively drawn to. There was also something about him that made me feel something that I had not felt in a very long time - the need to keep him safe. There was a certain sadness about him that I sensed - it was almost as if I could feel it somehow. It was my turn to talk now.

"Is this small island home for you?" I asked. He shrugged.

"I'm not sure about that." He brushed a few strands of hair away from his eye. He was so good looking. His dark hair was messy; it fell to about his jawline. He had dark blue oval eyes, a square jawline, a mouth that was a bit too feminine for a man, and a fair complexion for someone who lived on an island. His eyes were irresistible. They seemed to glisten when he spoke. He had no idea how beautiful he was, which only made him more appealing.

"Is this small island home for you, Kai?" he asked.

"I honestly don't know." I smiled. The moment I said it I knew it was the truth. I honestly didn't know what was in store for me.

My birthday was only a few weeks away. Land or sea, good or evil, mermaid or young woman? I didn't have the answers to any of it.

"I try not to think much further off than tomorrow. That is the point of living on islands like this anyway, right? The eternal buzz. Life's a beach, and all of the rest of it right?" I laughed.

"I guess so," he said. He took a sip from his glass. I could smell that there was a very good amount of gin in that glass. He pressed his lips together, closed his eyes for a moment, and looked at me thoughtfully. "Maybe some people just need to escape and start over. Everyone deserves a shot at redemption, right?" I nodded, I nearly lost my breath.

"Yes. Yes, everyone does."

Lee looked at me apologetically.

"I'm sorry. Did I say something wrong?" he asked.

"No. No, not at all. I've just been having a strange week. I have a lot on my mind, and what you said just makes sense," I said.

"You're an interesting girl, Kai."

"You're a pretty interesting guy, Lee." We both laughed. We talked for hours about our favorite places on the island, what kind of music we listened to, our favorite books, and our shared passion for art and poetry. I learned that Lee was from Chicago, and studied literature. He talked about how badly he wanted to be a writer even if he never made a dime. He had a great deal of published short stories, and had a few other notable credits that he seemed uncomfortable taking credit for. He came here to write without distraction, and create a non-complicated life for himself here. I didn't think I could possibly be more of a wrong fit for him. There was so much more to him that I couldn't wait to learn. I could see a dark sadness in those sapphire blue eyes.

"Were you running from something when you left Chicago?" I asked.

He smiled, and took a deep breath.

"I guess you could say that. The day I decided to leave I woke up one morning, looked in the mirror and realized that I hardly recognized the guy staring back at me. I didn't like him at all. I was in the shower washing away the scent and the sin of the night before when I decided I didn't like who I was turning into. There was a girl in my bed that I hardly knew, there were pieces of the night before that I barely remembered, and I was completely tired of self-medicating with booze and girls." He paused as if to make sure I was not going to get up and walk away. He smiled again.

"Yet here I am with a drink in hand, and a beautiful girl sitting across from me." He laughed nervously. "I don't know. I came here to get away from that version of my story. It's not me. It never was. I got a bit lost after I lost my parents, and I am slowly finding my way again." He threw his hands up in the air and smiled softly. "You can run now if you want to."

"I'm not judging. I promise," I said. "I get it." I did get it, and knew right there at that moment that I wanted to change. I didn't want to kill anyone ever again. I didn't want to hunt again. I wanted to be worthy of someone like Lee. I wanted to feel again. I wanted my soul. "I'm not running anywhere." I took the last sip of my water and realized I did actually need to run somewhere. "Oh my goodness! I actually do have to run," I explained.

"I knew it!" He teased. "I really do have to go, but umm….do you want to hang out tomorrow?" What was I even saying? I had no idea where I was going to be tomorrow.

"I can't," he said. "I wish I could, but I have to do some work around the island. It's kind of an all-day thing."

Oh good, I thought to myself. I didn't say that. Instead I said, "No worries. I understand." I got up to leave, and thanked him for spending the afternoon with me.

"I am so sorry I swallowed up half of your day. I have no idea how that even happened," I said.

"The pleasure is all mine," he said with a smile. "I rambled on so much about myself I think it's only fair that I listen to you ramble for hours. How about I meet you the day after tomorrow outside of the hotel about noon?"

"I'd love that." As I walked out of the bar I could feel his eyes on me the entire way to the door. I turned back, and gave him one last smile before leaving. The day after tomorrow it is, I thought to myself, and I couldn't wait to see him again. I felt like a human teenage girl again. It was exhilarating.

CHAPTER
Five

THE SUN WAS SETTING. I didn't have much time to get to Cleo, and I was truly afraid that she would do something terrible to show me just how serious she was about all of this. I couldn't risk that. There were a few people on this island that I'd prefer to see stay alive - and then there was the pesky little issue of not drawing attention to myself or anything out of the ordinary. Cleo did not strike me as the low-key type, so I hurried. I wanted to make a quick stop at the hotel before meeting her, mostly to check in on Adrian and Molly. There was something inside of me that would not stop nagging to make sure they were okay. What is going on with me?

As I approached the hotel I saw Cleo standing outside talking to Molly. I hurried over to them. Molly was wearing a pair of blue jeans and a red tank top. Her hair was pulled back in a messy bun. She looked so casual - she must have changed after her shift. She looked completely enthralled by whatever it was that Cleo was telling her.

"Hey guys. What's going on?" I didn't waste any time, and Cleo could clearly hear the irritation in my voice. Cleo spoke first.

"I was just asking Molly what was fun to do around here at night?" Molly looked at me and smiled.

"Kai, are you feeling better? I was going to see if you wanted to grab a bite to eat or something," she said.

Cleo's eyes lit up like the light of the full moon.

"I'm starved," she said with a wicked smile. I shot her a look of warning to caution her to stop testing me. She could read my thoughts anyway, and knew that I was moments away from ripping that gorgeous red hair right from her scalp.

"Thanks, Molly. We really do have to get going. We sort of have plans that we cannot get out of," I said.

"Oh okay." She said it with such disappointment, which typically would have irritated me - for some reason I felt guilty that her feelings were hurt.

"Later this week we will get that bite to eat," I said. That seemed to make her happy.

"Hey Molly, have you seen Adrian around? I wanted to ask him something about a flower I saw today." It was a flimsy excuse, but it was the first thing to escape my lips. I suspiciously looked at Cleo to see if her thoughts gave anything away. I got nothing.

"He left a few minutes before you got here," she said.

"Good." Molly looked at me confused. I smiled, and shifted my weight from one hip to the other.

"I just meant that we are kind of in a hurry anyway."

"See you later, Kai. It was good to meet you, Cleo." Molly turned to go.

Cleo smiled, waved, and shouted, "I hope we run into each other again soon!" We could not get this night over soon enough. The sooner she was out of town and my life the better off I would be.

"I could have killed her you know…It would have been easy. No one knows me here. Not that I care about details like that anyway," she said.

"Yes, I know. I want you out of here. Let's just go, and get this over with. Does she know I am coming?"

"Ava knows everything. Don't you get it?" The scary thing was, I thought I did get it. The truth was I had no idea what I was in store for.

The night air was cool, and the water looked amazing. The ocean was calm and shimmering like the stars were dancing on her surface. As we walked toward the shore I couldn't help but think about Lee. What was it about him that I was so drawn to? There was something about him that made me want to keep him safe. It was something I hadn't felt in a very long time. It was still a couple of weeks until the next full moon cycle, so it was not completely unusual to be having these kinds of feelings. My soul was intact - as much as it could be. Mermaids never had complete possession of our souls. Part of it belonged to the old ones. That was just the way it was. We had enough to feel love and compassion. We experienced emotions much like humans do - but our emotions are exaggerated; many of us choose to let go of what little grasp we have on the light we have inside, and embrace the darkness. After all, there were plenty of humans with souls that did terrible things all the time. I guess it was easier for us - we do lose all attachment to our soul during the full moon cycle. It's not all that hard to loosen your grip on it once part of it does return. Lately, I was feeling more of my soul than I had since before I turned. The past few months I'd been feeling feelings I forgot I had. The more I looked at the water ahead, the less things made sense. My birthday was next month. I wasn't sure if that was a blessing or a curse. I didn't know anything anymore.

"Are you nervous?" Cleo asked smugly. "You can feel what I am feeling. I'd assume you already know the answer to that," I said without looking at her.

"I can't make out your feelings. They are all over the place, and if I didn't know any better I would think I was listening to a human. It's tiresome. I am finished trying to figure you out. Totally…over…it"

"I didn't realize you were so interested. I thought you just wanted to come turn my life upside down before handing me over to my mother to get in good with her."

Cleo stopped walking, and grabbed my arm.

"No one gets in good with Ava."

I pulled my arm away from her.

"Then why are you doing this?"

She sighed, and sat down on the beach. I sat down next to her, although I was not convinced it was a promising idea.

"I have a debt to pay. I must serve her as long as she will have me. It is as simple as that." I looked at her, and then looked out at the sea. She quickly stood up, and darted me one of her glares. "I don't need you taking pity on me," she snapped.

"Good, because I'm not." And that was the truth. Cleo was dark. I could not sense any light inside of her anywhere - only darkness. I didn't know what her story was, and I didn't care to learn it. We reached the water's edge. The instant my foot touched the water I felt my chest tighten, and suddenly realized the magnitude of what I was doing. I felt a cold chill trickle down my spine like a drop of icy water slowly running along my skin. I was finally going to meet my mother. I started to turn around. I wasn't ready for this. I needed to try to reach Aunt Morgan before doing this. What was I thinking? How did I get here? I was turning around; to hell with the consequences. As I lifted my heel to turn around I felt myself slip into the water. I was being pulled under. She had me. She was there waiting all along.

I was pulled under so quickly. I didn't even have time to feel my legs transform into my tail. Everything was a blur of dark colors blending together. I was being pulled down further and further. This must be what sinking into quick sand feels like. I could hear the muffled sounds of panic from the creatures all around me. They were afraid for me. I could feel it. I'm not sure how long I had been descending deeper and deeper into the dark blue water. Was it mere minutes or hours? Time worked differently down here. It was hard to say. Finally, everything stopped. I was no longer being pulled. She let go.

I was dizzy, and disoriented. I could feel my mother in front of me, but I couldn't bring myself to look at her yet. I had imagined what she might look like so many times in my mind. I had spent years loving her and wanting her, followed by years of hating her and knowing that I'd never forgive her for leaving me. I was overwhelmed with emotion. I had no idea what I was feeling. I thought I was completely prepared to hate this creature. Everything I know about her is horrible. She is a monster. We were all monsters, though. Sometimes I forgot that I was every bit as evil and cruel as any other mermaid. The feelings that have been overwhelming me lately didn't change that. I caught my breath, and forced my eyes to raise to hers. I finally found the strength to look up at her. I gasped when I saw her. She was beautiful. She had long raven black hair, eyes that mirrored my own, and ruby red lips. Her tail was magnificent. It was black, and looked like it was covered in glistening black diamonds. Her long and slender arms were covered in black scales that almost made them appear to be tentacles. She wore a small single pearl around her neck that was strung through a thin rope. This was Ava. This was my mother. I knew in that moment I would do anything for her love, and to finally have her in my life. She knew it too. I could sense her feelings. I could not read her thoughts very well. It was as if something was blocking her thoughts from being able to be read, but I could feel something.

"What do you want?" I asked in a shaky voice. I was doing everything I could to not cry, scream, and laugh all at the same time.

"I wanted to see you face to face. I wanted to meet you, Kai. You have no idea how much I've missed you," she softly replied. Her voice was as soft and beautiful as delicate wind chimes ringing on a warm breezy summer day.

"I don't understand. I thought you didn't want me. I thought you lost your soul. Aunt Morgan said…" She stopped me right there.

"Morgan told you what you needed to hear to keep you safe. That's all. My sister had your safety and best interest in mind. She loves you very much."

I could not trust her. Even as I told myself not to trust her, I was fighting the words. I wanted to believe her. I wanted her to love me. That's all I ever really wanted. Every time I hunted, and took a life I secretly hoped she would find me. I secretly hoped our paths would cross, and she would beg for my forgiveness. I struggled with my own darkness for much of my life since I turned. I've always felt drawn to the darkness of what I was, and I always felt that it had something to do with my mother. In some strange way hunting and hurting people made me feel connected to my mother. It was the only thing I had of her, and in some disturbed way it brought me comfort. My Aunt Morgan could not stand by and watch me be so destructive. She swam every full moon cycle. Even as her soul separated from her essence every month she never behaved like a soulless creature. Part of me wanted to be exactly like that. I admired, and loved her so much - but there was another part of me that was drawn to the darkness. There was another big part of me that wanted to feel what my mother felt. I wanted to understand her pain, pleasure, and try to understand her. I flipped my tail, and turned my back to her.

"I have no reason to believe a word you say. You left me to live a life completely under the water; you left to live a life of power and self-indulgence. And now you demand my presence here weeks before my twenty fifth birthday?" I felt myself getting worked up. I turned back around to face her again. She didn't move a muscle. She was right in front of me. What was it that I saw in her eyes? Was that…understanding? She placed her hand on my shoulder. I winced, but I allowed her to keep her hand there.

"It is love and understanding that you see. I mean you no harm, Kai. I've left you alone for so many years because I wanted to see which path you would choose for yourself. You are my daughter, but you are half your father's daughter as well. I have great power. I have more power than any other mermaid in existence. There are things I can offer you. There are gifts I can share with you." I shook my head, and ran my fingers through my hair that was floating behind me.

I began looking around - really looking around at where we were. I'd never been this deep in the water before. We were far below the caverns and caves that lie near the bottom of the ocean. It was almost as if we slipped into another world under the already magical world that I knew. The water was a darker blue than I had ever seen. This would look like total darkness to a human. It was very cold; this was much colder than anywhere I had ever been. There was no shortage of strange and scary creatures lurking down here in the dark. Everywhere I looked I saw sea urchins, fangtooth fish, vampire squid, and many other creepy creatures that looked like they had swum straight from hell. Even I didn't like being in the company of fangtooth fish. They were small, but they were nothing to disregard. All they had to do was open their large mouths, show their enormous teeth, and suck their prey into their mouths. They were dull in color, had large lifeless eyes, and large razor sharp teeth. They were not well liked by any species down here. Of course, I did not fear them, but I didn't like them around either. They could not be trusted. Off in the distance I saw a volcano. Underwater volcanoes were beautiful when they erupted. It is like an underwater firework presentation - but they were also very dangerous. It has been rumored that there are cracks on the surface of the bottom of the ocean near the volcanoes, and that is where the old ones lived. From what I understood, none of us wanted to end up there. It was not unheard of for them to hold mermaids prisoner, harness their powers, and all sorts of other unpleasant things. If there was a hell in the waters, then that was it. My mother gave her soul to the old ones. She knew more about them than anyone else. She still hadn't really told me anything. It was time to get some real answers.

I rested on a large rock covered in dark seaweed and beautiful dark purple and black crystals. Ava waited for me to speak again.

"I'm not sure I understand what you mean. What kind of powers and gifts?" No sooner were the words out of my mouth did I regret uttering a single breath. Her eyes lit up, and her smile widened across her face.

"I can give you anything. You can rule down here by my side for eternity. You will be completely immortal soon. You are my only child, Kai. You should be down here with me." Oh my stars…I don't know why it had not occurred to me earlier. It's nothing I ever considered or wanted, but now that I knew it could never be I felt…loss. She could hear my thoughts.

"You will have to give up any attachment you have to any piece of your humanity." Why did this suddenly matter to me?

"But, Aunt Morgan still lived like a hybrid even after she became completely immortal."

Ava was anticipating I would say that. She was practically retorting before I finished my sentence.

"That was different. She had to raise you. It was required that she keep up that way of life until you were on your own."

I swam closer to my mother, "Are you telling me Aunt Morgan is here?" My heart practically burst out of my chest with happiness.

"Yes, she is. She does not care for this part of our world - she was never strong enough for it. She is under the sea, but will not come anywhere near here. She does not always approve of my methods. It's that pesky soul of hers," she said with a laugh. I was afraid of what the answer might be to my next question, but I went ahead and asked anyway:

"Did you hurt her?" Ava laughed hysterically. "Oh Kai. You have much to learn. Of course, I did not hurt her. She is my sister."

I shook my head in confusion.

"But I thought that…" my voice trailed off.

"You thought that I was a soulless monster capable of anything?" I didn't say anything. I didn't need to. She could hear my thoughts anyway.

"I suppose I am - but even monsters have their limitations."

"Will you tell me where she is? I want to see her."

Her expression softened.

"I'm sorry, Kai. I can't do that. She doesn't want to see you." I was holding back the tears now. There were hundreds of images flashing through my eyes of her. I missed her so much. She was the only family I ever knew, and now I find out she has cast me aside too. I always thought that we would see each other again and everything would be okay. I never imagined she could stop loving me, or no longer want to be part of my life.

"Why?" I asked.

"She hates what you have become. I'm so sorry, Kai. I know this hurts you, but I am here now. I love you for exactly what you are. You are part of me, and we are together now. Stay with me. Let me teach you how to use your power, let me share my gifts with you."

Just as I was about to rush into her arms we were interrupted. A stunning mermaid swam towards us. She had long wavy blonde hair that reached the start of her dark blue tail. She had sea plants braided throughout her hair, big bright blue eyes, and wore beautiful bracelets made from shells.

"What is it, Eve?"

"Cleo's debt has been paid. She is no longer of use to us. What would you like me to do with her?" Eve asked in a very cool and controlled voice. She looked me over. I heard her thoughts, and learned she knew who I was.

Ava looked at her and simply said, "Release her." Eve nodded her head.

"Very well," she said emotionlessly, and swam away towards the volcano. I realized that I had completely forgotten about Cleo since being pulled under. Before I had a chance to ask where she was going, I got my answer. I heard a terrifying scream that could only be described as a howling high pitched siren. She had given her to the old ones. Cleo's screams were sounds of a mermaid being stripped of her powers and tormented with the restoration of her soul. She was feeling every bit of pain she had ever caused anyone or anything. Ava swam back over to me.

"Kai, I can explain. You don't understand how things work down here." I didn't need to understand. I wasn't ready for any of this.

"I don't want to understand! I never should have come here!" I could not have swum from her and her strange underwater kingdom fast enough. I flipped my tail, pushed my weight forward, and swam faster than I ever had. I swam so quickly that I didn't see or hear anything around me. I wanted out of this water. I wanted the land, and I wanted to forget I had a mother at all. If only it were that easy. Eventually I began to slow down. I turned a corner around a large rock and saw something. I saw someone. As soon as I saw the first one, two more swam up behind her. I could hear their thoughts telling me not to fear them. After what I just experienced, I wasn't sure I could fear anyone any more than Ava. They knew who I was - everyone did. One was a female, and the other two were men. Mermen.

The mermaid was beautiful. She had a caramel color complexion, slightly slanted eyes, long wavy black hair, and a glorious gold tail. The men looked like Gods. They were both perfectly sculpted in every way. The first one had long blonde hair, electric blue eyes, and a dark green tail. He must have been 8 feet long head to tail. The second merman was just as beautiful. He had long dark hair, eyes as dark as the night sky, and deep blue tail. He was nearly the same size as the other.

The blonde merman spoke first. "I'm Isaac. He pointed to the other man.

"This is Liam, and that there is Liana. We mean you no harm."

"I know. I heard your thoughts. I would introduce myself, but it would seem that you already know who I am." The water was much calmer here. There were beautiful plants and flowers everywhere. "Is this your home?"

Liana swam closer to me. She smiled.

"The entire ocean is our home - as it is yours. But there are certain areas that we prefer to others." I nodded. Mermaids had a way of speaking in melodic like tones. Their words were strung together perfectly like a beautiful lullaby.

Liam moved closer to me and smiled.

"Kai, it is an honor to meet you. The daughter of Ava. I'm at a loss for words." I floated back to put some distance between us.

"I'm not sure I understand. How do you know who I am? Why have I never met any like us until now? I've been swimming for almost seven years." The words all came out much too quickly. I probably sounded like a mad woman.

It was Liana that took the first few questions.

"We rarely ever meet any others like us that live as hybrids. There are not many that live between land and sea. Most of us make our lives here in the water. We can visit the surface, but we do not leave the water. We all know who you are, because you are Ava's daughter. She has eyes and ears everywhere. The sea has been watching and protecting you all of these years. We all have. Your safety is paramount to Ava and her power. Regardless of what you may think of Ava, it is in her best interest to keep you safe."

"I don't understand," I said.

Isaac came closer and circled the water around me.

"You don't," he said. "Kai, you are a hybrid. You are half human."

I didn't understand what he was saying.

"We all are. We turn when we are eighteen, and then are given our immortality when we reach twenty-five. You guys just told me a few moments ago that we rarely find one another until we are given our immortality," I said.

Liana looked at Isaac. They were quietly agreeing that they were right to suspect I would not realize what they were trying to tell me. Now Liam was thinking that one of them should tell me.

"I can hear your thoughts. Can you please just tell me what-ever it is you are all quietly sharing?"

"Kai, you misunderstood what I meant," said Liana, "I was

trying to tell you that we do not typically meet hybrids, and that hybrids do not find us until after they are given their immortality. Once they choose to spend the rest of their lives in the water they find us. Most of us are not born hybrids. We are full blooded mermaids. Your mother's bloodline is one of the oldest, and most mystical. We never transform - ever. Your mother has hybrid blood - as does her sister, and any children that either of them have. It ends with you. You need to stay alive in order for her to keep her dark magic. If anything were to happen to you, she would lose everything and our lives as we know it would be forever changed. Ava may not be kind or particularly fair, but her existence and power maintains balance in the water. We remain protected and treasured. She is the gatekeeper between the creatures of the sea and the old ones. If that gate were to collapse anything could happen. She may serve them, but we all serve her."

Then something had occurred to me that I had never given much thought to before...

"I can be killed."

Liana nodded and confirmed my realization.

"Yes, you can - until your birthday. You can be killed."

I sat down on a bed of coral. Liam sat down next to me.

"Kai, everyone wants to keep you protected. Ava saw you getting closer to some of the humans above and thought it would be best for you to be down here with her - at least until your birthday. If the balance is destroyed down here it would only be a matter of time before creatures would be fighting over power, and our entire species could be overthrown and turned into slaves to some of the darker monsters that live in the shadows of the sea."

"But we are all monsters. Do you mean to tell me that mermaids don't kill humans?"

"We do what we have to do to survive. If there is a chance that a human can expose us - we kill them. Some of us are weak, and give into the pleasure that comes with drinking human blood for sport. Others never go up to the surface. You and your family are different. You have a more equal balance of darkness and light running through your body. You have the hunger and thirst for destruction, but then you feel the remorse from your actions - as a human would."

"What happens if I live the rest of my immortality out above?"

"Nothing. Everything remains intact as long as you survive."

She really did need me. It wasn't that she loved and missed me as much as she needed me to keep her power intact. I wondered if I was in any immediate danger from the creatures that would like to see balance destroyed. They all heard my thoughts.

"No. There are no creatures that could be a threat that are capable of having this information," said Liana.

That was comforting to hear.

"I would never do anything to hurt my own kind, but I do need to get back to the surface." My thoughts betrayed me and let them know I was thinking of Lee. They all shared a look of disapproval. "I'm not sure what any of my feelings mean right now, but I do know that something has changed lately. I need to figure out what that means." I did feel very connected to them right away, and this was what I've always longed for - friends of my own kind, a family, and a home. My Aunt Morgan was here somewhere, and I needed the chance to make things right with her again somehow.

Liam looked at me with understanding eyes.

"Let me swim with you then. I won't go to the surface; I'd like to swim with you."

"Fine." Liana and Isaac both were thinking that I was foolish, but they respected my feelings.

Liam swam with me as promised. He didn't dare get anywhere

near the surface, but he went as far as he promised. We both stopped swimming when we knew we were close. His expression was genuinely curious, and his dark eyes were full of intensity.

"What is it like?"

"What is what like?" I said. I knew what he meant. "Oh," I whispered. I hesitated for a moment. How could I possibly begin to put this into words?

"Try," he told me with his thoughts.

"It's all I know. The first eighteen years of my life, I spent as human. Then suddenly I was this completely different thing. I loved the way the ocean made me feel. The moon called on me as if I were her dark daughter. I felt powerful, and for the first time in my entire life I felt connected to something. Soon the hunt and the kill became like a hypnotic drug. I couldn't get enough. It took me away from the pain of not knowing my parents, spending so many years of my human life feeling abandoned, and cast aside. You know what feeding on a human feels like."

"Actually, I don't. I never had the desire to see, meet, or feed on human beings. They are just like an unknown animal to me."

"Oh." I couldn't hide my surprise. I assumed all mermaids were hunters and killers. "I suppose it is easy to become addicted to. Eventually the light and my humanity pushes the darkness out. And then I feel tremendous guilt and confusion. It's like having a foot in one world, and a fin in the other. I'm half animal, half human, and not very good at being either. The full moon brings madness and chaos to my everything. Is it that way for you?"

Now his eyes looked sad for me.

"No, it's not. I am this way all the time. The moon has no power over me. You have a darkness inside that comes from the old ones. It's a curse, Kai. It's not your fault. You have to know that." This was the most honest conversation I've ever had in my entire life. Liam smiled softly as he read my thoughts.

"I wish there was a cure," I said.

"Your mother could probably do something - but you must act with caution when dealing with Ava. Mother or not, she is dark and powerful. There is nothing she does without getting something in return.

"I'll remember that."

"Do what you need to do up there, Kai. But please know that you have a place down here. I'll stay close by so I can easily find you when you come back."

It was if I'd known Liam forever.

"Thank you, Liam."

"And, Kai?"

"Yes?"

"You must remember, it is a curse. It's not your fault. You were made this way, this is what makes you who you are. Once you stop believing that you are evil, you might be surprised at what you find." He turned, flipped his beautiful tail, and descended into the water.

"Goodbye, Liam," I thought.

CHAPTER
Six

IT SEEMED LIKE I WAS DOWN THERE for at least a week, but when I reached the shore, I quickly realized it was only about a day and a half. The light of the day told me that it was mid morning. The overcast sky prevented the sun from warming up the sand for my bare feet. The sun was being filtered by a blanket of grayish white clouds. My clothes were where they fell off when Ava pulled me under. This island was so unpopulated that I never had an issue finding my clothes where I left them. This time I was lucky by chance, but they were still here. I slid them on, and thought of Cleo for a moment. Whatever happened to her was not my fault, and she had admitted to killing at least three people here on the island. No, I would not spend a bit of my human fueled guilt on her. I started back to the Cliffside right away. I was eager to sit down and try to make sense of everything that had taken place over the last day or so. The mid-morning sun reminded me that it was getting closer to noon. Lee would be at the hotel soon. The sounds of the waves crashing against the shore left me more confused than ever. With each crash, I walked faster and further from the ocean until I was almost at the Cliffside. It was only a few more steps away. I snuck right past Molly in the lobby and made it to my room with time for a shower and change of clothes.

I showered and changed into a casual sun dress. As much as I knew I should have stopped to try to process everything that was happening to me, I didn't. If I could turn off my humanity when I hunted for the past seven years, then I could turn off my connection to my mermaid half for a day to embrace my human half. On my way out of the building I stopped and talked to Molly for a few minutes.

"Are you meeting up with Lee today?"

"I am. How did you know that?"

"It's a small island," we both said in unison. Molly laughed.

"Do you want to have a fire on the beach tonight? We might be able to see the turtles." I desperately needed to hold on to everything human about myself right now.

"Sounds great," I said. "I'll meet you out front around eight."

"See you later," she said with a smile.

"See you later."

Lee wasn't there yet when I got outside. Adrian wasn't outside either. I didn't think he ever took a day off. There was a stone bench in the garden in front of one of the rose bushes; I decided to sit there and wait for Lee. And there he was. His wavy hair was windblown, and all over the place as usual. He was wearing a pair of old brown cargo shorts, and a black tee shirt. He had his olive green Jansport backpack strapped across his back. He looked good.

"Hey. I'm sorry. Am I late?"

"No not at all. I had a head start. I live closer." We laughed.

"Well come on, I want to show you something," he said.

"Lead the way." We walked in the opposite direction of the Gator and other local businesses on the island. It was much quieter on this side of the island. We passed a few bike trails, and walls of trees. We stopped between two giant cypress trees along one the lagoons.

"This way." He led me toward a narrow path that was positioned between two massive lagoons. It was beautiful. There were egrets feeding, and alligators floating by. Every few minutes we would hear the shuffle of some small animal playing alongside the water. We were surrounded by nothing but green, and I loved it. It was a welcomed change from where I had spent the last couple of days.

"I come here a lot to get away from the noise," he explained.

"I can certainly see why. It's very peaceful."

"I'm thinking of building a small cottage or villa out here. Nothing fancy. I just want a place to chill out and disappear to."

"That sounds nice. Maybe you could start writing again."

"Maybe I could. What about you? Do you think you are going to stay here, or is this just a stop along the way?"

I really didn't know the answer to that.

"I'm not sure. Sometimes I think I will be moving on in another few days, and other times I think I could stay here forever." That was the truth.

"Well, you are kind of cool, and I like having you around. If that counts for anything." He winked, and walked ahead to catch up to a night heron he wanted to get a closer look at. We spent the rest of the afternoon talking about books we both liked, and music we both listened to. It was a wonderful day. I didn't want it to end. As we walked back he teased me about living like a gypsy in a hotel, and I gave him a hard time about being a wanderer on the island. We had a lot in common, and being with Lee made me feel like a human girl. When we reached the Cliffside, I was a little disappointed that our afternoon had ended.

"Hey, thanks for hanging out today. I like you. Is that lame to say? It sounds pretty lame."

"No. I like the way it sounds. Thank you for having me along today. I had a really nice afternoon." I couldn't stop smiling around him. We locked eyes for a second, neither one of us knowing what to do. I liked him. I liked him so much.

"Okay, so I'm going to go," he laughed nervously.

"Molly and I are going to a fire on the beach tonight. Do you want to come along?"

"Yeah…yeah, that sounds cool."

"Okay great. I think she usually goes near the pier."

"I know the spot. I'll see you guys later." He lingered for another moment. I gave him a quick hug, and waved goodbye. I ran into the hotel, and to my room like an excited teenage girl.

Molly and Lee were both waiting for me outside later. The air was cool and comfortable. Molly was wearing a pair of jeans and a purple tank top. She wore her hair down and wavy. She laughed as we walked and talked about how funny some of the guests were at the Cliffside. Molly had an energy that just made you feel good. She was always in a great mood. Her blonde hair, and tan skin made her look like someone straight out of a vacation commercial when you saw her skipping around on the beach. She was a lot of fun. I was glad I came.

"Kai, come on! You are falling behind." I was walking a few steps behind them. Watching Molly and Lee walk ahead so carelessly reminded me of how badly I wanted to be normal again. Lee looked over his shoulder, and waved his hand, telling me to hurry. I ran ahead to catch up to them.

"Sorry," I said. "I was just enjoying the night air."

"We have plenty of time for that," she said laughing, "look, everyone is over there." She pointed at the small group of people on the beach. I recognized a few of them from around the island. Terry the bartender was there with one of the girls that worked at the Gator. And there were a group of guys that Lee knew. They waved him over as soon as they saw him. He gave me a quick smile, and joined them. Molly and I walked over to another small group of people.

"Hey guys! Do you all know Kai?" There were two girls and a guy. The guy spoke first.

"Hey, my name is Bryan. I've seen you around."

"Hi," I said. The girls both smiled and waved.

"This is Anna and Tori," Molly introduced us, then walked over to mingle with the group of guys Lee was talking to. We all stood there for a few minutes in awkward silence. I decided to speak first.

"Have you both lived here your entire lives?"

Tori nodded and laughed. "Yep! Born and raised. Neither one of us have ever been anywhere else." I realized quickly that they were sisters.

"What about you?" Anna asked.

"I've only been here a few months - but I love it here. It's beautiful."

"Yeah everyone says that. If you were stuck here your entire life you would get tired of it." Anna smiled and bobbed her head back and forth to emphasize how true her statement was. I was about to respond when Molly came over and grabbed my arm.

"Sorry, I have to borrow her. Come on, Kai. I want to show you something."

Molly linked her arm through mine, and we walked a few steps away from the crowd. I smiled.

"What do you want to show me?"

"Nothing. I just wanted to pull you away for a second, and ask what was going on between you and Lee. He keeps looking over at you." I shook my head and smiled.

"I honestly don't know. We are just hanging out a little. That's all. Nothing really to tell."

"There is going to be something to tell. I can tell."

I looked over at Lee and saw him working diligently to get the fire roaring. He was arranging the logs so scientifically, I had to laugh. He looked up at me and smiled. Molly snickered. "I told you!" We walked back over to the group and joined the party. Everyone was very friendly. They all had stories to share of the island, and the tourists. Any time the topic of tourists came up I couldn't help but feel guilty. I had killed a few of them after all. I always tried to quickly turn the topic on to something else. It was a great night. We all sat around the fire, laughed, roasted marsh-mallows, and had a few drinks. Molly had disappeared with one of the guys from earlier. I couldn't remember his name. I know she had a bit of crush on him. And it appeared that the feeling was very mutual. I was starting to feel a bit spent, so I said my goodbyes to everyone.

"Hey, hang on." Lee ran over. "I can walk you back."

"Oh no, it's okay. You stay and spend some time with your friends. I'm totally okay. Really I am."

"What if I want to spend some time with my new friend, Kai?" He smiled sweetly, and extended his hand. I let him take my hand and we started walking back together.

"I guess you win," I said. He stopped walking and faced me.

"Look, I know we haven't known each other long, and I'm not really that guy that is looking for anything right now - but I like you. I really do. I don't want to pressure you, and I don't know what this is, but I know I want to keep seeing you. Is that cool? I'm not saying that we should get married, or even jump into bed. I just love talking to you. You're one of the coolest people I've met in a very long time." He stopped talking for a second, bit his lower lip, and rocked back and forth on his feet.

"I feel like I am saying this all wrong. Stop me at any time. I beg you."

"You're not saying it all wrong. I like spending time with you; I like you. I'd be perfectly okay with doing this again and again."

He smiled. He had such a boyish way about him that was irresistible. He brought his hand near my face, and brushed a strand of hair behind my ear.

"You're really beautiful, Kai. I think you probably know that, but I needed to put it out there anyway." He threw his hands up in the air and shook his head.

"You're so funny," I laughed.

We walked hand in hand back to the Cliffside. Our fingers locked together perfectly. Being around Lee made me feel more human than ever. Being with him made me want to be a better version of myself. Everything about tonight felt right. We both agreed we were going to take it slow, but we both knew things were happening fast. And it was exhilarating. When we reached the front doors to the building we both paused.

"Listen, I don't want to walk you up to your room because I don't want to come up," he smiled.

"I wasn't inviting you up," I said with a smile.

"I know. I know. I just want you to know that I think you are special, and I don't want to do anything to screw it up. I've both been there, and done that too many times. Live it, learn it."

"I know what you mean. Slow sounds good." I looked up at him, and we locked eyes. I could feel my heart tighten in my chest. I softly bit my lower lip, and moved my face in closer to his.

"How slow?" I whispered.

"Pretty slow," he said the words, and I felt his breath on my face. He moved his mouth closer to mine. For a moment, we just enjoyed feeling our breath on one another's lips and the build up to a first kiss. He brought one hand to the small of my back, and the other to the back of my neck. His hands were strong, but the way he touched me was so gentle. He touched me with such care. Then he softly pressed his lips to mine. He lingered there for a few seconds. Our lips slowly parted, and he kissed me with slightly more intensity. I could have kissed him forever. When we stopped kissing he brought his hand to my face, and ran his thumb across my cheek.

"Goodnight Kai. I'm going to want to do this over and over."

"Me too." He took my hand one last time then shook his head.

"Oh, I'm in trouble," he smiled. "I'm in trouble."

I didn't know what to say. I was always good with guys when I was hunting and seducing them, but I had absolutely no experience in falling for one. I said the only thing I could think to say, "Goodnight, Lee." He waved, and walked along his way. My entire body was trembling with excitement.

"I think I am the one that is in trouble," I said aloud to myself, smiled again, and went to my room to finally get some rest.

Lee decided to take the next couple of weeks off work. He told me he didn't have any work lined up for the week, and the last few jobs he did paid very well. He decided he deserved a break. I didn't have anything to do, so we decided to take a little staycation together. We spent nearly every day together. We would meet in the morning for breakfast and spend all day together. We were like two giddy teenagers. Some days we rode bikes on the beach, other days we rode along the lagoons. Lee showed me isolated areas near the lagoons on the island where we would sit and talk for hours. The last few days of our time off together we spent at Lee's place. His cottage was small and simple. It was situated along one of the larger lagoons on the island. There was an open floor plan that was light and airy. It was oblong shaped and flowed very nicely. At the rear of the room that acted as the living room area there were large glass doors that revealed a beautiful view of the lagoon. The walls were all light gray, and had very little decor. There were three large book cases that housed hundreds of titles. He had everything from The Hobbit to A Farewell to Arms. There was one large bedroom off the large room, and a medium sized bathroom.

Everything about Lee was interesting. We stayed inside the cottage and didn't do much at all. We took turns reading our favorite books together and listening to classical music for hours. He would lay with his head in my lap looking up at me as I read to him. He always chose Chopin for background music. Every so often, I would stop between sentences to look down and smile at him. I would twirl his dark hair through my fingers and stroke his cheek. We always sat on the floor. His carpet was thick and more comfortable than some beds I had slept in. It was a shade of ivory and looked brand new. He looked up at me and smiled.

"I wish we could do this forever." He reached one hand behind my head and pulled my face closer to his. We kissed. Our lips parted, but I could still feel his breath on my mouth. "Kai, I like that we are taking things slow. I do. But, I'd be lying if I told you I didn't want to know what was happening here." He pulled his head back and let it fall back on my lap. I shifted uncomfortably, and moved over a few inches. He lifted his head, and sat up next to me. I sighed. I didn't know what to say. I was hoping we would somehow skip this conversation long enough for me to figure a few things out. The moon would be full in a couple of days. I had to spend this cycle in the water. There was no doubt about that. My birthday was also in a week. Over the past couple of weeks I had been avoiding all of this. I wanted so badly to feel human that I wasn't thinking about being a mermaid. For the first time in a long time I felt human.

"I don't know."

"You don't know?" He raised his eyebrows, and grimaced. "Oh man, that's just great. I don't know what I thought you would say, but I hoped it was something a little more concrete than that." He shook his head in frustration. I reached out to take his hand.

"Lee, It's complicated. There is still a lot about me that you don't know. These past few weeks have been perfect with you - especially the last two weeks. I wish I could tell you with absolute certainty what that meant, but I can't. At least, not right now." Our eyes were locked. His eyes were so beautiful. I wish I could tell him everything, but I couldn't.

"Alright, I'm going to say something and I hope it's not too much. I know it has only been a little under a month, but I have spent more time with you and shared more with you than I have with girls I've spent months with. I think…" he paused, his hands were trembling, "I'm in love with you, Kai. I love you. I know it sounds crazy and I know I said we should take things slow, but I love you." My eyes filled up with tears. I held them back.

"Lee. I am falling for you too. I've never felt this way about anyone. I love you too."

He smiled, and came forward to embrace me. I stopped him.

"You and I are from two completely different universes. You could never love me if you knew what I've done, where I've been - what I'm capable of even now."

"Everyone has a past. You know I'm not proud of mine either." His expression was soft, his eyes were tender and full of love.

"This is a bit bigger than that."

"I don't care. It doesn't matter. I'm in love with you. I want you. I want to be with you. Kai, I've never felt as alive as I do when I'm with you. It was like I was just going through the motions before you came along. I was some robotic shell of the guy I used to be, of the man I wanted to be. You saved me." He grabbed me by the waist and kissed me with more passion than he ever had before. I was kissing him back with every bit as much passion. My hands were locked around the back of his neck and in his hair - he was grabbing my hips, then running his hands along my back, my waist, then over my back side. He smelled of clean sea air, and tasted like mint tea. His hands were in my hair now, and his lips were on my neck. There was a jolt of electric shock when I felt his tongue on my skin. He returned to my lips, and kissed me again. His left hand found its way to my breast, his right hand was on my back side. I let out a soft moan. I wanted him. My body was trembling with excitement. His eyes were full of intensity and longing.

"I can't wait anymore, Kai," he kissed me softly, "Are you ready? I don't want to rush you." I was ready. I didn't know what this meant for us beyond this moment, but I knew I wanted to be with him.

"I'm ready," I said in almost a whisper. He swept me off my feet and carried me into his bedroom. He laid me down on his bed, and stopped to look at me for a moment.

"You are so beautiful." He lowered himself on to me and kissed me softly. He pulled me up, and gently lifted my arms over my head to pull my top off in one quick move. He admired my body while he quickly unclasped my bra. He pulled his own shirt off, and kissed me again. We were skin to skin. I'd never felt closer to anyone. My body was aching for him. I'm not sure how long we spent entangled in one another kissing and caressing one another before he gently pulled my skirt and panties down. I pulled at his belt and unfastened his shorts. He kicked them off himself, then removed his boxers. He was breathing heavily. He stopped and caressed my face with his hand, he paused for a second.

"Are you sure?"

"Yes." I wrapped my legs around his back, and held on tightly to his strong shoulders. We made love. Our bodies connected on a level that felt spiritual. We made love three times that afternoon, then spent the rest of the day lying in bed laughing and worshiping one another.

The bedroom window was open which allowed a gentle breeze to come in. We listened to the sounds of birds chirping, and trees rustling outside. The air smelled as if it was going to rain soon.

"Let's never get out of this bed," I smiled, laughed, and nuzzled my head into his chest.

"This is nice." Lee was running his fingers through my long hair. He kissed the top of my head, and twirled a strand of my hair around his finger.

"I love you," he said, "You are not going anywhere." I lifted my head to look up at him; I smiled and crinkled my nose.

"I'm not going anywhere." I meant it. I didn't want to leave the comfort of his embrace. I never wanted this feeling to end. I realized how impossible that was, but there had to be a way. I thought of Liam's words when he told me Ava may have power to keep me human. I also remembered his warning about the danger of making deals with her. I couldn't think of Ava and her conniving plans right now. Right now I was with Lee and the rest of the world could stand still. And it did, until the phone rang. Lee hit the ignore button on his phone, and set it down on the table next to his bed. It rang again - and again.

"Man, what can be so important?" He reached over and grabbed the phone. "Hello." He sat up quickly, and put his hand over his forehead. "What? When? I can't believe it." I sat up quickly, and started pulling my clothes back on. I could hear the words on the other end of the line. It was Terry. "Oh my gosh. Thanks for calling, man. Alright. Yeah, you too." He set the phone down next to him and looked at me. I knew what he was going to say before he could get the words out. My heart sank. "That was Terry from the bar. Molly is dead. She drowned a few hours ago."

CHAPTER

LEE SAT THERE IN SHOCK for a few minutes. Suddenly, the warm breeze and light sounds of the birds chirping were replaced with cold dead silence. My heart sank. I knew immediately that this was my fault. If there was one thing I was sure of, it was that this was at the hand of Ava. It had to be. Lee's chest rose and fell with every deep breath he took. His dark eyes were full of pain.

"There will be a service tomorrow at the Pier, then I guess they are having some type of thing at the Gator afterwards. I can't believe this is happening. Why would she have gone out at high tide? Molly is a local girl - she knows better." He looked at me searching for something in my face to make him feel better. I put my hand on his shoulder.

"I'm so sorry, Lee. I know you guys were friends. I don't know what to say." I sighed deeply and shook my head. "She was so sweet," I said. I meant it. Molly was the only girl on this entire island that made any type of effort to be my friend - as much as I tried to keep my distance, she never stopped trying. And now, because of me she was dead. I looked at Lee, and suddenly faced the reality that I had put him in danger as well. I couldn't have known this would happen, yet here it was happening. Everything around me was caught in a whirlwind of chaos that I had no control over.

This was a glimpse of what life on land would be if I chose humanity, or perhaps this was her way of telling me that I'd better do exactly what she wanted. Lee's words snapped me out of my own thoughts.

"Hey, you okay?" Could he see the guilt splattered all over my face? Could he see the guilt, the shame, and the darkness covering my entire body?

"I'm not. I'm sorry…I need to go," I said

"Right now?"

"Yes, right now."

"Are you going to the service tomorrow?"

"I can't think about that right now." I got up and ran straight for the front door, never looking back. I ran all the way back to the hotel. I ran as fast as I could without drawing attention to myself. The voices in my head were drowning out every other noise around me. Images of Molly unfolded in my mind in the form of a slideshow. Guilt and shame overwhelmed my mind, and my heart. Who pulled her under, I wondered? Was it Ava, or did she have one of her servants do her dirty work for her? She did give Cleo the ability to come to land to get me - killing humans in the process. Could it have been Liam, Isaac, or Liana? There was no one I could trust. My heart was beating so fast I thought it would burst out of my chest. "Why!" I screamed. "Why are you doing this to me?" Tears ran down my face, this was all my fault. How could I let this happen? I never should have come back to the surface. Never.

The plan was to get back to the hotel, check to make sure there was nothing in my room that should not be there, and leave this island for good. Lee was not safe as long as I stayed near him. The full moon was days away, and shortly after that I would become immortal anyway. It was foolish to imagine I ever had any actual choice in my future. Any dreams I had were never truly meant to become anything but that - a dream, a dream that hours ago I thought I held in the palm of my hand. Too much damage has been done. I had committed far too many evil acts, caused too much destruction to ever have a shot at anything pure or good. This was my reminder of all of that. This was my reminder of what I was, and where I came from.

Adrian was sitting on a bench in front of the hotel when I arrived. His hair was a mess, he looked like he hadn't slept in days, and his eyes were red from crying.

"She was a good girl. She didn't deserve this," he said very slowly. I stood in front of him, and nodded in agreement. I realized then that I hadn't seen him in weeks.

"I know you didn't want this, Kai." He spoke in a very flat and controlled voice. His hands were lightly clasped together, and he was slowly putting one over the other - then again.

"No, I didn't want this." Why would he say something so strange? He looked up at me with accusing eyes. No - he couldn't possibly know.

"I know what you are. I wasn't certain at first, but I figured it out little by little."

Panic washed over my entire body.

"Adrian, you're upset. You're not speaking logically. I'm sorry."

He stood up, and grabbed my arm. I pulled away quickly. This couldn't be happening. I didn't want to hurt Adrian. I felt my blood begin to stir, I looked off towards the ocean calculating how quickly I could get him in the water before anyone could see me. I could do it. We were moments from sunset. Now it was my turn to grab his arm.

"I'm sorry, Adrian," I said in a cool and quiet tone.

He gently placed a hand on my hand that had a grip on his

other arm. He must have known I could kill him. How could I possibly risk exposure? Our eyes were locked. Adrian's glare was every bit as determined as mine was. He was not cowering away. I couldn't sense an ounce of fear from him.

"Kai. You don't belong here. I need you to go before anyone else gets hurt. I can see the glow in your beautiful eyes. I know what it means. I've lived practically on top of the sea my entire life. I spent years sailing out there. I know the legends." He paused, shook his head, looked out toward the ocean, then back at me once again. "I met one like you long ago. She almost destroyed me." His words stung. I immediately let go of his arm, and jumped back. I looked at him more carefully than I ever had before. I let myself relax and curbed my natural instinct to protect myself and destroy him. I thought very carefully about what my next words would be.

"What is it that you think you know, Adrian?"

"I think you know the answer to that, Kai."

"I want to hear you say it out loud."

He stepped closer to me and leaned close to my face. He whispered, "m-e-r-m-a-i-d."

There was no use in denying it. I could use magic on him if I needed to, and I suddenly wondered why no one had if he claims to have met one.

"How could you possibly know, and yet still be alive to speak of this?"

"Because she loved me, and I loved her more than my own life. I would have given my last breath for her, and almost did."

Now my heart was pounding, and I was fighting back all of my tears. I could never hurt him. Oh god....how could I not have sensed this? Goose bumps covered my arms; I nearly lost my breath.

"Kai, I don't want to hurt you. I see softness and tenderness in you. But, this isn't right. Innocent people get hurt when your kind come into town. I…err…" his voice trailed off. I was stunned by what he was telling me. Could he be my father? This must be the reason I was so drawn to this island. I sat down and sighed loudly. "Adrian, I didn't hurt Molly. I would never have brought any harm to her."

"I know. I know. And I know you can kill me right now if you wanted to, but I don't think you will."

"I'm not going to hurt you. There is too much to explain right now, and I do have to leave. There are so many things you don't understand," I paused to take a breath, "I'm not sure I understand how you know of mermaids, and were permitted to live?" I asked in a cautious tone. I didn't want to frighten him with my question.

"I don't know. I still don't think I really understand any of what happened all those years ago." He sat down next to me and rested his hands on his thighs. "I met her one day while I was out taking pictures of the dolphins strand fishing. I dropped my camera in a tide pool," He laughed, "I am many things, but graceful ain't one of them, that's for sure. Anyway, when I kneeled down to grab it, there she was. She was the most beautiful girl I had ever seen. Her eyes were almost identical to yours. She looked like she had stepped off a movie set or something. I thought they were filming something here or they were doing a modeling campaign. I didn't know - all I knew was that I'd never seen a girl like her before. Her hair was long, dark, and wild. Her skin was as smooth as the inside of one of the seashells on the beach. I never thought love at first sight was possible until I laid my eyes on her, and I've never loved anyone since."

"What happened? How did you find out what she was? How

did things end between the two of you?" I didn't mean to ask so many questions all at once, but the words rolled off my tongue like dominos.

He smiled softly, and looked off toward the ocean again. He appeared to be lost in a dream.

"After a few weeks of seeing each other I proposed to her. I knew it wasn't logical to do it so soon, but I wanted to spend the rest of my life with her. I told her I wanted the rest of my life to start at that very moment with her. She cried and cried. Finally, she told me what she was. Of course, I thought she was out of her mind, so she showed me that night. When I saw her as a mermaid I fell even more in love with her - it was like being under a spell. We made plans to marry, and I fooled myself into thinking that would work somehow. A few nights later we were on the beach…" He shifted uncomfortably on the bench, and took a breath, "We were, err you know, enjoying each other's company, and she changed."

I sat up a bit straighter on the bench, I knew what his next words would be but I asked him anyway.

"What do you mean, she changed?"

"She went mad. She attacked me. I don't know what came over her. She screamed and cried in a voice I barely recognized. I'd never in my life, and never have since seen anything like that. She screamed and pulled at her own hair, she dug her fingernails into her skin and clawed at herself like a wild animal, then she suddenly stopped. She looked at me told me that she loved me, and that she was sorry. She ran towards the water, and the last I saw of her was her tail flip once in the air splashing water behind her."

"I'm sorry, Adrian." My heart hurt for him, and it hurt for Lee. My heart sank a little further in my chest, and it hurt for me too. I knew the words he spoke were true, and that Lee and I would most likely have a similar fate. "She couldn't control herself. The force of the moon had too strong of a hold on her," I explained quietly.

"I know. I figured it out over time. For a while I became obsessed with trying to find her. I learned all I could of mermaid legends and myths. I read folk lore, literature, tried to study art...I did everything I could to spend all of my time dedicated to her. Eventually I started wondering if it had been magic, or if I imagined the entire thing. I moved on, but I never forgot about her - my Ava."

I gasped. I didn't mean to have an actual physical reaction to hearing him say the words, but I lost my composure for a second. Adrian quickly looked at me, and I saw a glimmer of hope in his eyes.

"Do you know of her? Is she alive out there somewhere?"

I shook my head, and rested a hand on his shoulder.

"I'm sorry. I gasped because I've never heard a story quite like yours, and I'm afraid I am facing a few hard truths of my own."

"Lee," he said.

"Yes," I whispered. "But I am leaving. I won't put him through what you endured. I won't destroy his chance at happiness."

"Kai, she didn't destroy my chance at happiness. She showed me what true happiness with another can be. There was no other human girl that could have ever measured up to that after her. As much as it broke my heart when she left me, I wouldn't trade a moment I had with her for the world. I still hold on to hope that someday I will find her, or some evidence of her again."

He knew nothing of her being pregnant. He didn't know I existed, and I couldn't put him through anymore pain. In this moment, all I was certain of was that I had to leave.

"I trust you will keep my secret?" I asked.

"Of course. I have for all these years, haven't I?" I didn't conclusively know the answer to that, but I had to trust him.

"I suppose you have," I hugged him, and held on to him a few seconds longer than I should have, "I'll go. Goodbye, Adrian."

"Goodbye Kai. I wish we could have stayed in one another's lives a little longer." It was nearly impossible to hold back my tears now. The words he uttered meant more than he would ever know. I wish we could have as well, I thought. I really did. Instead of saying any of that, or trying to elucidate any of what I was feeling I smiled softly, then turned and walked away. And just like that I was losing one of my parents all over again. It would seem I would find myself orphaned over and over in my lifetime - this time didn't hurt any less.

The moment I entered the hotel I felt the despair; it was almost as if you could see the sorrow polluting the air in the form of a thick blanket of dark gloom hovering above. The silence was beyond silent - the sound of your own breathing sounded as loud and intensified as an alarm or siren. No one spoke, and no one smiled. It was as if Molly had taken all of the warmth and happiness with her when she died. Without her standing in the lobby chatting about cheerfully, or helping someone while laughing, the hotel was just a cold building. It was still beautiful, but it had become hauntingly beautiful. Molly was such a part of this place. I guess I didn't realize it until now. My heart sunk - I felt the weight of it in my own chest. This was my fault. There was no question of that. I didn't kill her, but she would still be alive if it weren't for me. There was nothing I could do to bring her back or make any of this any better to anyone here that loved and lost her. The only thing left to do was to leave - now. Everything around me was perfectly still. I passed one of the housekeepers in the hallway. I could never remember her name, but she was always quite pleasant.

She hummed to herself while she worked, and always stopped to say hello. She said nothing today. Her eyes were bloodshot from crying, and she didn't say a word. Everyone in the building had that same look. The sooner I left this place, the better off everyone would be. The keycard to my suite was not working properly. Sometimes I had to insert it in the door several times for it to work. If I became frustrated enough, I would simply take it to Molly at the front desk and have her slide it through her little electric device to reactivate for me. She would remind me not to keep it near anything in my wallet that had a magnetic strip on it, and we would laugh together knowing that I likely would anyway. That would never happen again. I turned to put my back against the wall and slowly slid my way down to the floor. I brought my knees to my chest and buried my head. My shoulders rose and fell with every sob I let out. Images of Molly, Lee, and Adrian all ran through my mind.

"What have I caused," I cried aloud, "What have I caused?"

After crying for Molly, the realization of the life I could never have, and everything else about my humanity, I stood back up and slid my keycard slowly into the slot on my hotel suite's door. It worked this time. I sighed, and walked into the room. Looking around at everything here was sobering. It was time to get a hold of myself, control my emotions, and focus my energy on the one who was truly responsible for all of this - Ava. There was nothing here that was suspicious or that I was concerned about being discovered once I left. My clothes and personal belongings were all neatly put where they belonged. I gathered everything and packed it all away nicely in a few bags. There were a few rocks on the dresser that I had gathered from one of my walks with Lee. The rocks served as painful reminders of everything I was not going to have, and of everything I was giving up. When I picked up one of those rocks and rolled it between my thumb and index finger I let myself remember how hard I fell for Lee, and how quickly I fell for him. I thought about taking one of the rocks with me, but put it back down on the dresser. For a second I thought of calling him and saying goodbye. It would be far too difficult to try to say goodbye to him, and even more difficult to try to explain why I was leaving or where I was going. No, I needed to make a clean break. My human heart felt as if it were breaking into a million pieces inside of me. This was much more painful than I ever could have imagined. The only comfort I found was in knowing that leaving was the only way I could keep Lee safe; it was the only way I knew Adrian would be safe. If I loved them - truly loved them, as humans love, then I had to let them both go. I finished packing my things, and left a note instructing the hotel to donate my belongings to whichever local thrift store or charity they chose. I also left two envelopes. One of which was to be delivered to the shop girl from the boutique that I first met back on my first day on the island. It was a greatly delayed tip for her services that day in $1000 cash. The other envelope was to be delivered to Lee. Inside the envelope was a letter from me, and one of the small rocks.

Dear Lee,

I'm sorry that I left you in such a hurry today. I suppose the news of Molly was overwhelming, and my head was a complete mess. I reacted abruptly without giving anything much thought at all. I'm so sorry. I hope you can understand, and know that you didn't do anything wrong. I wish I had the courage to call you, but I guess I'm not as strong as I'd like to believe I am. The truth is, I must leave. I realize that my timing could not possibly be worse, and I'm sorry to leave you when there is so much sadness on the island. Please know that I will be thinking of you often, and I wish I could be there with you every day forever. A family matter has come up, and I must go home. I can't be more specific than that. Thank you for some of the best days of my life. Our summer together will always be magical and precious to me. I know it was only a month or so, but it felt like I'd always known you - and that you were made just for me. I meant every word I said to you. I hope you do remarkable things, Lee. Please don't be angry with me for this forever. Thank you for showing me what love feels like - what it looks like. Thank you for letting me fall in love with you. Thank you for loving me back.

Kai (always yours)

I put everything in the corner of the room, and left my key-card. It was time to go - well past time.

Leaving was the right thing to do. It wasn't fair, but a young innocent girl just lost her life - I was in no position to be considering what was or was not fair to me. Leaving the hotel without drawing attention to myself was easy. There were not many people in the hallways or lobby, and those that were here were grief stricken and completely unaware of anything happening around them. As I walked out of the hotel I looked back at the desk where I had first met Molly. Where she once stood now was a portrait of her surrounded by flowers and candles. And all because she unknowingly befriended a mermaid whose mother was an evil conniving sea bitch. I could feel the hatred driving me closer to the ocean. Suddenly I couldn't wait to dive in the water and confront the one responsible for destroying everything I had here.

I ran toward the ocean. My feet slid over the sand beneath me. I ran so quickly that all the human eye would see would be a blur of motion. I didn't care about the risk of exposure at the moment, I just wanted to get in the water as quickly as possible. The full moon was approaching. The gravitational pull from the moon was starting to present itself to me. There was no time to undress or think about anything. There was only time to dive and crash into the water. The instant my head was under the water I felt all of the darkness within myself come to life. My clothes fell off as my tail emerged. I pushed off further into the water with my tail and felt myself descend into the deep dark waters of the ocean. The water was warm at first, and felt like silk against my cool skin. I glided quickly through schools of other fish, ducked under jelly fish, twisted and turned through caverns and caves, and made my way through tangled plants and seaweed. I was determined not to slow down until I reached Ava's lair.

The water began to feel cooler. This meant I was getting closer. The color of the water was also getting darker. It was beginning to take on a blue-black tone. Gone were all the beautiful and brightly colored fish and sea creatures. Gone were the colorful flowers and plants I so loved under the sea. All that were in these waters were dark hideous looking creatures. Moray eels were lurking around hoping to find unsuspecting sea dwellers to feast on. They knew to stay away from me. I could tear them apart in less than five seconds - and I would. They were quite intimidating looking creatures, and very scary. They even had an extra set of jaws in their throats with teeth. They were about thirteen feet long, with large black button shaped empty eyes. Some were red, some were gray, and some were green. Their disgusting bodies were covered in mucus that contained a toxin that could be fatal. They were not very well liked. One Moray had his eyes on me, and slithered closer to me as I swam. I snapped my head towards him, and hissed. He slithered away. As I swam along I passed an array of terrifying looking creatures. Sea snakes, squid, sharks, and even stone fish all were common dwellers in this part of the water. Stone fish were particularly nasty creatures. They looked like any other rock on the bottom of the ocean. They were true masters of disguise, and incidentally the most venomous fish in the world. Their venom causes paralysis, and eventually death to their victims. Mermaids were immune to that venom. We couldn't be killed, but we could still feel the pain of the venom. In some cases, we could even become temporarily paralyzed. Luckily, they were not known to attack mermaids - but I have heard other sea dwellers tell stories of mermaids that became paralyzed when a stone fish felt threatened over the years. They all kept their distance. I could communicate with them all, and knew that none of them wanted to bother or be bothered by me. I asked if anyone knew where my mother was. One goblin shark told me I was very close to her. I thanked him, and moved along. How long had I been swimming, I wondered? Could it have been days? Time moved so much differently down here. I felt the moon. It must have been at least two days. I should have found her by now. She must know I am seeking her out, I thought to myself. I saw something coming towards me. It was still far enough away that I couldn't tell what it was in these dark waters. I was at the bottom of the ocean. It was nearly black down here. The glow from the volcanoes off in the distance offered some light, but nothing substantial. I could hear its thoughts, and knew right away who it was. It was Eve. It was the mermaid that had executed Cleo's sentencing a few weeks ago.

"Oh come now, you don't really feel badly for Cleo, do you Kai?" She smiled a wicked grin and moved her hands gracefully as to keep melody with her words. I didn't feel badly for Cleo. She was suffering horribly for all the destructive things she had done to others. As far as I was concerned she deserved it. She didn't kill humans because of any curse. She did it for pure delight. She made a deal with Ava to be able to walk in both worlds, much like I can, simply to deliver me to Ava. The only reason she could have possibly wanted to live on land was to murder humans. I couldn't sense a soul anywhere on her when I encountered her.

"Your thoughts are precisely correct, Kai. She does deserve to suffer, much like you think that you do - but you don't deserve to suffer as Cleo does. You are different. You are special."

Eve and I were face to face now. She reached out and grazed my face with her hand and smiled softly. I cautiously backed away a bit.

"Just because you can read my thoughts does not give you any insight to who I am. Let's not pretend that you and I even know one another," I snapped back at her.

"Oh, I know you. I know you very well. And I know why you are here. You want to hurt Ava for hurting your human."

"For hurting her? She drowned her. That girl posed no threat to anyone and you all know that."

"What difference should that make? Do you suddenly forget all the lives that you have taken? Did they pose a threat to us? How is that any different? Because you suddenly started feeling badly about it after killing how many human men?"

She was right. My god, she was right. I wasn't any different than Ava.

I looked away, then looked back at Eve and asked, "Did Ava kill Molly herself?" I was afraid of the answer.

"No. She didn't. She sent Cleo to use magic on her, convince her to come to the water at high tide, then controlled the water to drown her. It was Cleo's will to do this for Ava to have her soul taken away once again. Little did she realize that Ava only had her soul replaced after she did her bidding," she laughed, "The deal was never meant or said to be permanent."

"Yes, I've heard that making deals with Ava is not something to be taken lightly."

"I suppose not. Although, there are instances where it works out for both parties. It depends on your perspective," she said as her hands danced along to her words.

"Are you here to take me to her?"

"I am."

"Do you know how long I have been swimming?"

"Three days." She could sense my thoughts, there was no reason to ask my next question.

"Your birthday is in three days' time." She grabbed my hand, "Follow me."

I let go of her hand, and swam beside her as she commanded. Eve's long blonde hair trailed behind her like a beautiful silk scarf. She was stunning. She had plants and flowers braided through her hair. The last time I saw her she used only plants. She was certainly dark and she served Ava, but I didn't feel contempt for her the way I did upon first meeting Cleo. Besides, all mermaids served Ava in one way or another. Liam, Isaac, and Liana had all confirmed that. They all agreed that Ava in position keeps balance under the sea. She serves the old ones, and everyone serves her. They all believe it is a small price to pay to keep the mermaids safe from evil creatures and dangerous sea dwellers.

"Are we close?" I asked.

"Yes. Can't you feel her?"

"I don't feel anything but anger."

"Focus."

She was right. I could feel her; I could sense her presence. And just like that she was right in front of me.

Her green eyes sparkled as brightly as a beautiful new emerald. I hated that my eyes looked so much like hers. There was nothing about her that did not disgust me in this moment. She swam closer so that our faces were only inches apart.

"My deepest condolences about your human friend, Kai. What a tragedy," she whispered. It was as if she had just slapped me across the face. Without realizing it, I balled my hands into fists, hissed, and revealed my fangs. I whipped my tail at her with every bit of force I possessed. Clearly, I was no match for her, but I didn't care.

"Her name was, Molly," I hissed. She moved her arms so quickly I didn't see them until I felt both of her hands pressed firmly down on my shoulders. With one quick lunge, she forced me to the bottom of the ocean, and held me there.

"If you are quite finished, child," she said in her melodic tone.

My eyes darted up at her, and then all around to determine what my chances were of getting out of here in one piece. They were not very good. Eve stood behind her with three other mermaids I'd never seen. The three mermaids were not like other mermaids I had encountered. They were positively evil looking, and identical in every way. They all had long wavy white hair with thin black streaks throughout the color, pale white skin, and bright yellow eyes. Their faces reminded me of an owl; it must have been because of those large, round, yellow eyes. They were surrounded by sea snakes, and had large black tails with scales I'd never seen before - their scales were tiny little knives. The damage these three could do must be limitless. These mermaids were predators, there was no doubt about it. Their thoughts confirmed all of that. I could hear the mermaid in the middle warning me to stay right where I was. To the right of Ava were three large eels, and to her left there was a large goblin shark showing off his giant yellow fang like teeth. I thought of screaming for help, but there was no one down here that would help me. I wriggled under her hold for a moment, but quickly realized there was nothing I could do but let whatever was going to happen here happen. I spent my entire human life wondering where I came from and longing to know my biological parents, and for what? To find a father that could never know of his daughter, and a mother who truly was a sea monster. My Aunt Morgan was right to shield me from Ava. She warned me. I wondered if she knew this day would come? Some mermaids have the power to see the future. Perhaps that is why she decided she could have no part of mine; maybe this was my future. I held back my tears of pain, disgust, and anguish. Ava would not get a single one of my tears. Not now. Not ever.

"Why are you doing this?" I said in barely a whisper.

She loosened her grip on my shoulders, and slowly moved her hands away from me. She spun quickly, and ran her fingers through her long black hair. She used an index finger to twirl a strand of hair around and around.

"Oh Kai. Kai, Kai, Kai," she sang. "I needed you to see the price of choosing to live as a hybrid. Humans will get hurt. You will hurt them. What sort of life would that be for my daughter?"

"But…you killed a girl that posed no threat to any of us," I shouted. I know I have done much worse myself. I've not forgotten, but I was ready to change. I don't want to hurt anyone ever again. I don't want to bring about destruction. I would have swam every full moon - without question. That was my decision to make." I was losing control. I hated how controlled and poised she was.

"Be that as it may, your decisions have a profound impact on far more than you realize. You become immortal in less than three days. Choosing to live an existence on land with some human puts us all at risk of exposure. You must know that. You will lose control eventually. It is in your nature. How long did you hunt and kill before finally giving in to your humanity, and fighting your darkness?" She swam in another circle, then positioned herself in front of me again. "I serve the old ones. There are rules down here."

"I am not you," my chest was rising; I floated up so I was no longer sitting, "Don't presume you know anything about me." Our eyes locked. She knew what I was thinking. She knew about the conversation I had with Adrian, my father.

She looked away into the distance, her expression became more thoughtful.

"Then you know that I almost killed your father, and I would have. Then you must know that you will kill your human mate as well."

I shook my head furiously.

"No...no I wouldn't."

"You do not possess a full human soul, Kai. If you did, the crimes you have committed in your past would destroy you. You will eventually lose control. It is part of the curse on our blood line."

Ava reached at the pearl necklace around her neck, and let it lie between her fingers for a moment. She looked at Eve and then the three sisters and motioned with her hand for them to leave.

"Leave us," she said. The four mermaids, the eels, and the shark all swam towards the volcanoes away from us. "I was very much in love with your father. Much as you are with your human. I wanted more than anything everything that you think you want right now. It simply isn't possible. I left him to keep him safe, and even after that he wasn't safe. He was not safe from me. I was obsessed with him. I'd watch his every move. I'd watch him from down here through this," she held her pearl in her hand again, "It's a mirror of sorts," she explained. "There were so many times I was tempted to pull him into the tide, and under the water with me. I wanted him near me so badly - I could have destroyed him in a blind moment of passion and love." She stopped for a moment, and looked thoughtfully at me. "I had to forfeit my light and every part of my soul to the old ones so that I could move past those human feelings I had. Those feelings that caused me to be weak, and not in complete control of myself. I made a deal. That is that. Part of that deal was letting Morgan take you once you were born. I've watched every moment of your life through this pearl," she brought the pearl to her lips and softly kissed it. "I have been there for every moment of your life waiting for your twenty-fifth year to finally come - for your immortality to come so that we could finally be together. I will not stand by and watch you try to turn yourself into something you are not. You are my daughter. You must feel that." I was a bit lost in her words. She had explained so much. This was too much to take in at once.

"Why would I believe a word of this?"

"Because you know it is the truth. I am certain that you do. I know that as much as you want to believe that I am a horrible monster, you realize that everything you are is because you and I are connected. The temptation, the pull to the water, the need to hunt, all of it. Kai, you may have lived as human for most of your life - and you may have lived as a hybrid for some time, but you have always had one foot in the water. And you always will."

Everything was spinning out of control. The dark water slowly began taking on another form. It was circling around me in a dark, slow, moving, blur. A dark vortex was sucking me under, and I couldn't move. I couldn't move! I wanted to scream, but I couldn't find my voice. My heartbeat was slowing down, bump.....bump....bump... I thought I heard screams of panic in the background. Sounds were completely muffled now. The last thing I remembered thinking and perhaps saying before falling into complete darkness was, "I'm not immortal yet. I can be killed." Then there was nothing but the darkness.

CHAPTER

WHOOSH, WHOOSH, WHOOSH. That was all I heard. Whoosh, whoosh, whoosh. Everything was still completely dark. Had I died? There was no physical pain; I felt nothing. These are my thoughts, I must be alive. There was ambient noise and perhaps muffled voices in the distance, but no sounds were clear. I was drifting in and out of consciousness. My mind was certainly playing games with me. I saw Lee. He appeared so lost and broken. He was sitting by the giant oak tree where I had first seen him. He sat there staring out into the ocean as if he were looking for answers.

"I'm sorry, Lee," I said, "I never wanted to cause you pain." He looked angry and hurt. His hair was in tangles, it looked as if he hadn't shaved in days, and his clothes were wrinkled. My heart hurt for him. Then I saw Molly, she was still alive. I saw her with Cleo walking towards the water at high tide.

"Molly, stop!" I yelled. She couldn't hear me; none of this was real. I watched her get pulled under by the current. I could sense that her mind was numb in a magical haze; she wouldn't have felt frightened or even struggled to fight for her life. She would not have felt a thing. None of this brought me any comfort or peace as I watched the waves throw her small lifeless body back to the shore. Images of Adrian working in the gardens flashed before me. He seemed older, and a bit more worn than I was accustomed to seeing him. He wore gardening gloves while he pulled weeds from the earth. He stopped, removed one glove, and wiped the sweat from his forehead. He sat down on the bench where we had our last conversation. The sparkle that was normally in his youthful eyes was gone. Mourning the loss of Molly has brought up all his painful memories of Ava. I wasn't sure how I could hear all of their thoughts, but I could. I wish I could comfort him. I wish I could tell him I was his daughter and try to make up for some of the pain my mother had caused him. Then I saw Ava. She was holding a baby in her arms. She was kissing the baby's forehead, and telling the child how much she loved her. She was sobbing uncontrollably, she looked so hurt.

"I love you. I will never let anything happen to you. I will love you if they take every bit of my soul and light away. I will still love you." She held the child tighter, and rocked her back and forth. She looked as in love with the child as any other new mother, perhaps more. How could it be that I was having these visions? I could see the past and the present. My gift was magic and mind control. I didn't have visions. Unless that was something new...

The water moved slowly and steadily. The earth seemed to be breathing in and out with every rise and fall of the rippling waves. I was floating, or at least I felt like I was floating. It could have just been the movement of the water around me, and the ambient noise making me feel as if I were floating. I could feel! I could not feel very much, but there was a sensation of motion that I was aware of. The muffled voices I heard earlier were becoming clearer. It was Ava's voice that I recognized first.

"Is she going to survive? She frightened one of the stone fish, and they got to her before I realized what happened."

"Why would Kai have frightened the stone fish?" The sound

of the other female voice was very familiar, but I couldn't recognize it clearly yet.

"Her emotions were running very high. She was livid when she made her way to me. It was pure rage driving that girl through the water to find us. Then her rage began transforming into pain and confusion. Her emotions and energy put everything around her on high alert. A mermaid with Kai's power on overdrive will do that. You know that. I'm keenly aware of just how much you love blaming me for all things that go wrong in this world, and the next."

"Hmm…And what did you expect she would do after you killed her human friend and forced her back to the water? Really Ava, that was an incredibly manipulative and calculated move even for you." I felt the woman's hand run across my forehead. It felt familiar and comforting.

"You know as well as I do that it needed to be done. I do not create the rules, but I must enforce them. What choice did I have?" Ava's tone was intensified, she was nearly shouting.

"You always have a choice. You should know that better than anyone." The woman let her hand linger on my face for a moment, "She will be fine," she said as she gently pet my head, "I've healed her."

"I'm grateful. My power under the sea is nearly limitless, but for when it comes to my own daughter." *Was that defeat I heard in Ava's voice?*

"Kai is immune to your dark magic. There is only one thing you can give her, and that is something I can't imagine you would ever give."

I wish I could see them, but the tone in both of their voices told me that they were both very emotionally engaged in this conversation. I couldn't feel their thoughts. I was not fully conscious yet.

"Why would I give my only daughter the one thing that could destroy her? I do not need to justify myself to you, Kai is my daughter. She is mine, and despite what you might think, I do love her without limit."

"You have no soul, you have no light left in you," she laughed, "You rule the ocean with a dark heart, and almost never show mercy of any kind. You cannot love - anyone or anything. You may be worshipped, but it is driven from fear." She sighed, "You forget that she lived as human longer than she has lived as a hybrid. It is her life, Ava. Not yours."

"I'd watch my tongue if I were you," Ava said coolly, "Don't think for an instant that I would not have it cut out. The only reason I let you live your life outside of all of this is because of Kai. You kept my daughter safe, and I suppose I owe you yet again for saving her now. Do not tempt my darkness that you are always so eager to discuss and try to make me swallow like shards of glass. You may have raised her, but I am her mother."

Aunt Morgan. It was Aunt Morgan. Of course, it was. I had heard once long ago that she was a healer. She did still love me! She did still care. My eyes began to open. I blinked rapidly until I could focus. There she was sitting beside me and holding my hand. She sensed me waking up, and quickly began comforting me.

"Shh, easy beauty," she said with tears in her eyes. I began breathing regularly and moved my head slowly to make sure that I had regained control of my body again. Her thoughts were clear now. She was wondering if I was completely healed. I nodded my head to confirm. I wanted to speak, but I had no idea what to say, or who to say it to. Ava swam above me and kissed my forehead,

"I will leave the two of you. I suspect Kai has many questions for you, sister." Ava looked at me one more time before vanishing.

"I'm sure you have many questions, Kai. Right now, the only

thing that matters is that you are okay. Regardless of what you think, I will always be here for you. I distanced myself from you because you needed time to discover who you are, and who you want to be. I never stopped caring about you." She smiled.

"I've missed you."

"I've missed you too," I said. I still felt a bit weak. "This is all a bit overwhelming for me." I slowly began to sit up. Aunt Morgan helped me as I found my strength again. We locked eyes, and I threw myself into her arms. I cried like a child, and let her rock me back and forth. My entire body rose and fell with every sob, much like the waves of the ocean. "I'm sorry," I cried, "I'm so sorry. I wish I could take it all back. I wish I had the strength to live as you did, and do. I would give anything to have that kind of control - but I don't. I never did."

"Shh," she soothed, "Kai, it's the curse; it's not something you ever had a choice about."

"Then why did you distance yourself from me? Ava told me you hated what I had become."

"I had to. There were things you needed to discover and learn for yourself," she petted my hair and smiled softly at me, "Enough talk of sadness for one day. Today should be a joyful day."

I scanned her thoughts before she had the opportunity to speak again. I knew what she was going to say, but I let her say it anyway...

"Happy Birthday, Kai."

I felt my eyebrows raise, and I sat up a little straighter. It felt like someone had just jolted me awake from this dream I was having. Only it was no dream, and if it were my birthday then that also meant something else...

"When do I become immortal?" I asked in an emotionless tone.

"When the sun sets. It will be done," she smiled, "You won't feel anything like you did when you first came of age and changed. You will simply feel a deeper connection to the sea - you will feel your energy change. It's very subtle, and happens so quickly it is over almost as soon as it begins. This is a big day for you." She swam up so that she was in a standing position. She slid her hands to rest on the top of her tail, where her human hips would be, and shook her head back and forth. "You are all grown up now, beauty. Your future is yours to control." I looked up at her with a blank stare. The ripples in the water seemed gentler somehow. The ambient noise seemed softer.

"I'd like to be alone for a bit; I'm happy you are here, but a few moments of solitude would be nice."

"Of course. I will let Ava know that you are entirely healed," she looked up and rolled her eyes, "That will please her." I could sense the animosity and resentment she felt for Ava. She was covered in it.

"Thank you, Aunt Morgan." She looked at me one last time. I could sense she was trying to figure me out in that moment. Then her thoughts quickly jumped to another place; she was wondering if I could find my way around in here.

"I'll be okay," I said. "I've been in plenty of underwater forests before."

"Of course, you have. I will see you later, Kai." She swam away gracefully leaving little bubbles in the water as her tail swayed behind her.

I blinked slowly a few times, then looked down at my hands and studied them for a moment. I thought of all the pain these hands have caused. These hands were evil, but at the same time I couldn't help admire how smooth and beautiful they were. How could something that looks so delicate and beautiful be so bad? Schools of colorful small fish swam past me. The forest was very peaceful. Everywhere I turned there were plants and giant kelp that provided homes and safety for many sea creatures. The water was very clear here which confused me a bit, because I thought I must be close to Ava's lair. The area I was in was closed in by canopies of kelp, plants, and large rocks. It was very peaceful. There was a beautiful garden full of sea plants and flowers surrounding the large flat rock that served as a resting spot. Some were bright yellow and shaped like stars, others were rich aubergine with petals that resembled soft spikes. There were exotic blends of brightly colored, budding bouquets all around me. It was a glorious sight. The plants and flowers gently swayed with the ripples in the water. As they moved slowly back and forth, I ran my fingers along them. As I ran my fingers along the delicate plants, I reminded myself how capable these hands were of nurture and goodness as well. I had loved Lee, and treated him with care. One thing was certain, I was through feeling sorry for myself. What's done is done; there was nothing I could do to rewrite history or change the things I've done. If that meant I had to spend eternity haunted by my remorse and shame, so be it. When I was out from the venom of the rock fish I saw things - I saw things that had already happened, and things that were happening in the present. My thoughts quickly darted to Lee. He was in so much pain. I had to go to him, somehow. My heart ached for him. I swam back and forth, pacing. My senses told me I only had a few hours until sunset. It was impossible to get back to Lee that quickly. There was too much to try to process right now, between Ava, Aunt Morgan, my immortality, Lee, and everything else happening. I had to take on all of this one crisis at a time. I flipped my tail, and swam through my dwelling. I swam through the plants and kelp looking for Ava. The clear blue water was very easy to navigate through. The sea plants didn't get in the way as much as I had feared they would. After swimming for a few moments, I sensed I was no longer alone. I stopped near a sunken statue from the surface. The statue was chipped and worn, but still very large and quite impressive. It was a man and woman dancing.

"Lovely, isn't it?" Ava asked. I straightened my back, and brushed the hair out of my face with my hand.

"Yes. It's lovely."

Her voice was smooth and softer than I'd ever heard it, I wondered if she was feeling badly about the fact I had nearly died.

"Did your quarters suite you well?"

"Yes," I nodded slowly and let my shoulders relax a bit. "Thank you for taking care of me, and for calling on Aunt Morgan to heal me."

"Did the two of you have time to chat?"

"We did. She explained some of what I needed to know, I guess." My eyes lowered to the surface below us.

"She and I do not exactly have a close relationship, but I am grateful that you had her - have her."

I laughed a little like a mad woman for a few seconds. My emotions were rising and falling with the waves.

"I have no idea what I have or had. I'm not sure any of that matters. Happy birthday to me."

Ava's eyes lit up, she didn't seem to notice I was falling apart.

"Yes, happy birthday to you! Do you know what this means?"

"Immortality?"

"Yes."

"And my soul?"

"What of it?"

"Do I get it back now?"

Ava swam closer to me and took my hand. I allowed her to lead me, and I swam alongside of her. I couldn't read her thoughts right now.

"Where are we going?" I asked her.

"You need to see something so that you can understand things."

I swam silently along, not questioning her again. Why didn't I question things with her the way I probably should? Was it because she had power over me, or was it more basic than that - did I want to obey? We glided through the water swiftly and gracefully together. Every creature we passed cleared a path for us the moment they saw or felt us coming in their direction. I could feel her power and position here as we traveled through the sea. I could feel the fear and respect that everything around us felt for her. We swam through another beautiful forest, a couple of caverns and caves, and then through open water until we were in darker waters again. It was colder, and the water looked almost black. The volcanoes were in front of us, and I knew that this must be part of her lair where I first found her.

"Come," she said.

I followed her as she glided closer to the volcanoes. She must have felt my hesitation, she finally spoke again.

"The volcanoes won't harm you. I've frozen their activity so we can pass through safely." She certainly did have powerful magic. It made me feel more at ease all the same. We came to an area completely swimming with eels and sharks. They cleared an opening for us, and she stopped near a large sunken ship. The ship was split in two, covered in coral, and frozen in time. I could see the winding staircase was still intact through one of the windows. It was another ship on the floor of the ocean that vanished beneath the waves the way so many things do. I thought about the hundreds of lives that were likely lost in an instant, and wondered if their lost souls were down here with us. I thought we were going to go through the ship, but we didn't. We stopped right in front of it. There was a large flat stone on the floor that she slowly slid over without ever touching it. She truly controlled everything in the sea. Once the stone was out of the way, it revealed an opening that could only be described as a hole in the floor at the bottom of the ocean. I knew in that moment that we were going in, and we did. I followed her head first down the hole at the bottom of the darkest part of the ocean with no idea of what to expect. Nothing ever could have prepared me for what was beneath the surface.

CHAPTER
Nine

As we swam down the dark hole I realized we were passing through some type of secret tunnel. It was pitch black, and completely silent. Once we reached the other side of the tunnel there were two mermen in full armor that served as guards. They both had blood red eyes, long white hair, and very muscular upper bodies. Both had jet black tails covered in spikes. They reminded me of the creepy white haired female sisters I met earlier. These two also had snakes wrapped around their arms that looked every bit as terrifying as they did. As soon as they saw Ava they nodded and bowed to her. She shot them a hard glance with her bright green eyes, and said nothing to either of them. I stayed right beside her. As we swam past them I really began to look around. The water was a dull muddy blue color, and it was very still. The moment we submerged into this world I knew that this place was something horrible, but I didn't know how horrible it was. My eyes darted back and forth from left to right. Everywhere I looked was horror and pain. There were mermaids chained up and screaming as if someone was torturing them. Sounds of sirens all around. There was another mermaid caught in a small whirlpool - only the whirlpool was a vortex of fire. She screamed and screamed. I couldn't see what she looked like - only the flames. I shuddered and winced. This couldn't be real. There were other creatures that I didn't recognize that looked like a cross between a human and an octopus. They had tentacles, but human like faces. Some of them were trapped and tied up in vines looking lifeless and tortured, and some were made to work as slaves. There were creatures that were made to suffer as shark and eel fed upon them as they screamed out in pain, and there were other mermaids that looked fairly normal that obviously worked as guards here.

"Is this hell?" I asked.

"It is one of the hell dimensions," she responded in a matter of fact tone. "I want you to pay close attention to the merfolk we passed at the beginning. The ones that scream out in terror in chains; those mermaids are lost causes who made deals to have their souls restored, then went mad because of it. They all end up doing terrible things, and risk our exposure which ultimately leads them here. The old ones always see that any threats to our kind live out their immortality in torment here. "I cannot risk that happening to my only daughter. I cannot restore your soul."

The shock of where I was, and what I was seeing was still settling in. I didn't respond right away, and when I did it was completely unrelated.

"Are some of those creatures human, or were they human once?"

She looked into my eyes, and then looked off into the distance. I knew she was not going to answer me. Perhaps I was better off not knowing anyway. My skin was crawling like I was covered in thousands of sea worms. My chest felt tight, and it was getting harder to breathe underwater.

"The old ones are down here with us. They can feel how powerful you are going to become, Kai. Don't do anything to give them a reason to put you on their radar more than you already are." I nodded knowing that I had no other choice but to say and do what I was told. "They have my soul, and my light. They are responsible for every bit of my power. I serve them. I need you to understand that there is a command that is to be respected, and there is a balance that must be maintained." And with that she offered her hand to lead me back to the tunnel so we could swim out of this hell in water.

We passed more tortured souls and creatures on our way out. Some of the guards stared at me intensely as if expecting me to act out of turn or do something foolish. As if I would even blink down here. This was a place of true evil. This was a place that monsters and demons feared. I couldn't get out of here fast enough. I was following behind Ava now, staying as close to her as possible. Her dark hair flowed behind her so beautifully. I had to wonder if I looked as magical as she did when I was gliding through the sea. I was trying to focus on anything other than what I was surrounded by. We were back at that tunnel, swimming through to reach the other side again. I was actually happy to reach Ava's lair. The dark waters, volcanoes, sharks, and eels all looked like heaven compared to where we had come from.

Once we reached a cave nestled between two of the smaller volcanoes Ava slowed down.

"Follow me, Kai. I'd like you to come into my home." We swam through the small opening of the cave and entered her home. Of course, she had guards at her gate as well, but her guards did not look like they swam straight out of hell; they were beautiful. There were at least a dozen mermen guarding her home. They were all muscular, God like, and gorgeous. They all held spears and shields. Each of the mermen had turquoise tails and wore thin ropes around their necks with a shark tooth attached to it. They all nodded to her with respect as we passed through. Once we were inside of Ava's cave I was amazed. I bit my lip to hide my excitement. This was an underwater castle, hidden within a cave. It was if I had found the lost city of Atlantis. She threw her head over her shoulder to see my reaction. My eyes were opened widely, and my mouth had opened and locked in a gasping position.

"Do you like it?" She smiled, and laughed. "The forest and garden you were in earlier is actually attached, there is a separate entrance but you can get there this way as well." I didn't reply to her, instead I just followed her through the enormous cave. I never would have guessed how massive this place was by looking at the opening from the outside. That is part of the magic of the ocean, nothing is ever what it seems to be. My shoulders relaxed a bit as we swam along the grounds. My breathing finally felt natural again. Whatever Ava was, however evil she was, being here with her was heaven compared to the hell she just showed me. Everywhere I turned there was some bit of wonder and beauty to admire. There were huge shimmering purple and white stones dangling from the sides of the caves and rock that served as sources of light. They reminded me of magical icicles. The water was the most beautiful shade of blue I had ever seen. There were seats and furniture made of shells, enormous bamboo, and coral. There were pieces from the human world here as well. Ava had impressive collections of chests and jewels. When we reached her chambers, I think I had finally hit sensory overload status. She had a throne, but it wasn't any throne. There were beautifully carved stone steps leading up to a landing that supported an enormous sea shell that was opened so that the bottom served as a seat fit for a Goddess, and a large curved back. On one side of her throne was a statue of a mermaid, and on the other side was a large piece of shimmering corral surrounded by flowers and colorful plants. Ava gracefully took her place at her throne. She commanded so much power with every move she made. It was at this moment that I finally realized how powerful she was. It was also in this moment that I realized everything she told me was true. Our eyes locked as she sat there gazing at me with love, and I felt more connected to her than anything I'd ever felt in my entire life. She felt and heard my thoughts and smiled at me.

"I can't tell you how happy it makes me to see that you finally see things as they are, Kai," she said in her normal controlled melodic tone. "Do you also see now why I cannot restore your full human soul?"

I looked at her and wondered if I could be happy here with her forever without ever returning to the surface. The memory of Lee's face flashed before me, and I knew that I couldn't. I did feel connected to her, and there was a strong part of me that wanted to remain under the sea with her forever. There was another part of me that would know I would always long for Lee and a life on land with him. I ran my fingers through my hair and shook my head.

"There must be a way I can have both."

"There isn't."

"How do you know I will go mad as others have? I am your daughter, perhaps I am stronger than the others."

"Kai, you are stronger than the others. You are also much more powerful than you can possibly understand in this moment. You will go mad. You will risk destroying your human, yourself, and you will pose a risk to our kind. I cannot allow that to happen. I will not allow you to ever be in any jeopardy of being taken by the old ones."

"Can't Aunt Morgan heal me if that happens?"

"It doesn't work that way. I'm sorry."

"So that's it. I can't be with him?"

"If you return to land, then you will live as you have lived since the day you turned to hybrid. You will feel the pull of the curse with every full moon cycle, and you will live without your full soul. Can you do that?"

"I could still live as a hybrid?" I'd never really considered that before. I believed that once I reached my birthday and received my immortality I would have to live as one or the other. I thought Ava and the old ones would see to it that I had to choose. I thought I'd be under water forever. My heart started racing, and a dozen questions began filling my head. *Could I do that? Could I live without hunting on land? Lee would grow older, and I never would. How would I survive all of that emotionally?*

Ava nodded her head and blinked slowly, "If that is what you want, then yes." She paused and looked at me with a worried expression, "You will still risk hurting him, and you will go back to a life that you were desperately trying to escape. Is this human worth it?"

He was. I knew he was. I couldn't believe what I was hearing. I never thought she would allow this to happen. Then my thoughts went to Molly. She died because of this, because of me. Ava used her as a permanent and painful reminder of what choosing the life as a hybrid meant. There was a big part of me that hated Ava for it, but I also understood this was the reality of what we were.

We were interrupted by one of Ava's subjects. He swam in without looking at anything but the surface below him. Then he looked up at Ava, and quickly bowed his head.

"I apologize for the interruption," he said, "It is almost time, and Morgan is here." Ava looked as if she had been anxiously waiting for this announcement.

"See that the grounds are secured and send her in," she commanded.

"Yes, of course," he said. He swam away, and a moment later

Morgan was swimming towards us. She looked at me and smiled.

"Are you ready?"

"Is it time?" I barely recognized the sound of my voice. Suddenly I was very nervous, which didn't make any sense considering I had known this moment was coming for many years. How could this still be the same day? The events that had taken place from the time I awoke from my comatose state until this moment seemed like days. I knew that it would happen quickly, and I would not feel much. Aunt Morgan had prepared me for that. I knew this wouldn't be the painful and intense transformation you read about in vampire or werewolf novels.

Aunt Morgan came to my side and placed a soft hand on my bare shoulder.

"It's time," she whispered. I always knew this time would come, but nothing truly prepares you for immortality. I didn't spend any time thinking about whether or not I wanted this; I never had a choice. Instead my thoughts were darting back and forth about what this meant, if I would feel any different, if I would finally receive my full scope of powers, and how I would live out my immortality. Ava raised from her throne and swam to my other side. She slowly pulled her pearl necklace from around her neck, and put it around mine. It felt cool against my skin, and I felt a quick shock of energy when she let it fall into place on me. She gestured with her hand for me to take a seat on her throne.

"There is nothing to fear, Kai. Take your place at my throne for your moment." I did as she instructed. I cautiously sat down at my mother's throne. I half expected something crazy to happen the second I sat down - but it didn't. *So far so good,* I thought. Ava took one of my hands and Aunt Morgan took the other. They both stayed by my side, then they both surprised me when they joined hands forming a circle. Ava began softly singing words I didn't understand, then Aunt Morgan joined in as well. The water around us formed a strong whirlpool. They both grasped on to my hands tighter while they continued singing. The water continued to stir around us; our hair was flowing above us tangling and twirling around. All I could hear was the sweet sounds of their bewitching voices and the water swishing loudly. I eventually closed my eyes as everything had become a giant blur anyway. I felt it! It was happening! I felt myself become one with the sea in a way that I've hadn't felt since the night I first turned so long ago. Every thought left my mind, leaving it clear and wide open. I was falling deeper and deeper into the sea - plunging towards underwater tides. I was buzzing with energy all over, and then everything fell into slow motion before I came to a rest again.

My mind settled back into reality and I opened my eyes. Ava and Aunt Morgan were both still holding my hands. We were all positioned the same way we were before I closed my eyes. I felt as if I had taken a wild and exhilarating ride, but I had been sitting here the entire time. I felt strong and peaceful at the same time. My mother spoke first.

"Happy Birthday, my sweet girl." She had tears in her eyes.

"Thank you, Ava." I hated her, I loved her - it was all so very complicated in that moment.

Aunt Morgan ran her hand across my cheek. She looked at me and softly smiled.

"I am very proud of you, Kai. I must go, but you will always know how to find me now." She leaned in to kiss me on the cheek, quickly said goodbye to Ava, and turned to swim away. She turned her head back once before going, she could hear my thoughts wondering what she meant by what she said a second ago.

"Your necklace, Kai. It will all make sense before you know it." She smiled, and then she was gone. I reached my hand to my throat and pulled at the pearl necklace Ava put around my neck. The moment I touched it, I knew it was mine. Ava sat down next to me at her oversized throne. She stroked my hair and just looked at me for a few minutes.

"You look beautiful, Kai. You wear immortality very well. The sea is yours to rule with me if that is what you want. Let's discuss what happens now…"

CHAPTER

Ten

I SPENT THE NEXT FEW DAYS with Ava, allowing her to teach me the secrets of the sea and the history of our kind. It was all fascinating. She explained how we could keep our existence a secret for so long, and when the folklore and stories began circulating about mermaids and sea people throughout history all over the world. It seemed that every country and culture had their own theories and tales of mermaids and sea dwelling creatures. Some of the stories had bits and pieces of truth mixed in with the myths, and others were completely inaccurate. The one thing all the tales had in common was that we were spotted. That was true. Humans had interesting ways of comforting themselves when they experience something that simply cannot be explained. Of course, humans could never truly know of our existence. They would try to destroy us. I already knew that. Some humans were fascinated with the idea of mermaids. We were romantic and mysterious creatures that represented sensuality and allure. Others thought that mermaids were wicked creatures that seduced sailors with our songs, only to pull them under the sea. The truth was, they were all a little bit right. Mermaids have been used on land in art and literature for as long as anyone could remember. To some we are nothing more than fairy tales, and to others we are wonders of the sea just waiting to be discovered. Ava made it very clear how important it was to protect the secrets of the sea. I was forbidden to ever speak of our secrets to any human for any reason.

Ava took her time explaining most of it, and finished my lessons with the story of our creation. This was nothing that Aunt Morgan had ever shared with me; I was a very captive audience when she began speaking.

"Mermaids were here long before humans were. All life comes from the sea. It is the ultimate source of life and power. Mermaids were goddesses created in the perfect image of the old ones." She paused for a moment, and smiled because she could read my thoughts. "This was long before there was any talk of Amphitrite and Poseidon. This was before good and evil existed. According to legend the mermaids lived in harmony together for hundreds of years before humans came into existence. There were only three of them, and they were immortal. Their names were Marella, Ula, and Kaia. When one of the mermaids first encountered a human, she became obsessed with him. Eventually, her sisters became obsessed along with her. The old ones adored their goddesses, and eventually gave in to their desire to collect this mortal man. The three sisters lured him into the water with their beauty and magic. As he went under the water with them he slowly transformed into a merman." I was afraid to interrupt her, but there were so many questions running through my mind. Ava answered the two most important ones in her next few breaths. "Mermaids have endured the thirst for humans ever since. They each shared him, and eventually started to have offspring. He ended up choosing Kaia to spend his immortality with. His name was Morgan." I knew what she was going to say next before the words escaped her mouth, "They had two daughters, Ava and Morgan." I brought my hand to my mouth and raised my eyebrows. Ava paused for a moment before continuing. She was giving me a moment to take all of this in. I nodded at her to let her know I was ready to hear more. "Marella and Ula were mad with jealousy; they combined their powers to curse Kaia and Morgan as well as their offspring for eternity. They cursed them to an existence of not truly belonging to either world as hybrids, and to have a dark thirst for destruction at the force of the full moon. That it how the curse began.

"But I thought the old ones cursed our blood line?"

"It began with the sisters. Much has happened since then, and the old ones have played a very significant role in all of it."

"What happened to Kaia and Morgan?"

"The sisters found dark enough magic in their jealous hearts to steal their immortality. According to legend they turned them to sand so they could never be together again."

"What happened to Marella and Ula?"

"They became too powerful, and no longer cared about the rules of the sea and serving the old ones. Eventually the old ones removed them from this world, and put them in another."

Confusion was beginning to set in again, and as usual my head was racing with questions. I was suddenly remembering what Liam and Liana told me about our curse and dark magic. They told me that the old ones cursed our blood line, and I needed to stay alive in order for Ava to keep her dark magic. Of course, Ava was listening to my thoughts. She broke the silence once again.

"Kai, there are very few mermaids that actually know the true story of creation. Some of what they told you was true, and some things were left out. They were correct to say I needed you to stay alive until you reached your immortality to keep all of my dark magic. I hope you have come to realize that there was more to me wanting to keep you safe than my power."

"I have," I said.

She smiled and stroked my hair. Ava had a softness to her despite being the most powerful dark creature of the sea.

"Good," she quietly sang.

I turned from her, and rolled my pearl between my thumb and my index finger a few times.

"I also haven't forgotten that you are evil, and you have done horrible things."

She smirked.

"I could say the same to you, Kai. The only difference is, I don't feel remorse as you do. You wouldn't have to either, if you chose to stay here with me."

I knew she was right.

Despite my better judgment, I stayed in Ava's kingdom for a few more days. I explored the grounds, and spent a good deal of time in my own quarters. The cavern was far enough away from everything else here that I truly felt like I was in my own little world under the sea. My gardens were beautiful. I was surrounded by beautiful rocks, crystals, and colorful coral. There were some trinkets and sunken treasures from above strategically placed as decor. There were a few smooth, large rocks to sit on, and my bed was a huge circular shaped shell surrounded by flowers and plants. Eve came in most days to check up on me. She would bring small meals of plants or small game, offer to comb my hair, and see that my gardens were taken care of. I never imagined she was going to be responsible for personally serving me. One day I finally asked her if it bothered her. Eve had just brought me a bowl of small shrimp. She put them on one of the rocks, and asked me if I needed anything.

"This can't be fun for you," I said.

"Fun?" She laughed, "I'm not interested in fun, Kai. I am grateful to serve Ava and have a place in this kingdom. Now that means serving you as well."

"Well, I don't need to be waited on," I said.

"Of course, you do, Kai. Like it or not, you are the daughter of the most powerful mermaid under the sea. You are the envy of many."

I looked at Eve for a moment and wondered if she and I could ever be friends. Eve winked at me, then quickly brushed her blonde hair away from her shoulders.

"Let's not get ahead of ourselves princess," She sang, "I know that you don't trust me. I wouldn't trust me either, but I do make a good friend. And let's face it, princess, you could use one."

I smiled. Maybe she was right. I wasn't sure that I was ready to start sharing secrets and braiding one another's hair, but the idea of having another mermaid to spend time with was nice.

"I'll check in with you later, Kai."

"Thank you," I said.

Eve smiled, and left. I looked at the shrimp, and decided I wasn't hungry. I combed my hair, and decided to go for a swim. I didn't want to see Ava, and had been doing very well avoiding her. I knew she wouldn't hurt me, and I knew that she loved me in her own dark twisted way. I just wasn't sure I could stay here. Before I left the grounds to find open water, I played with the pearl that hung around my neck. Suddenly I was remembering the words, "It's a mirror of sorts." It was time I figured out what this pearl did. The pearl felt smooth and cool between my fingers, I closed my eyes. I let my mind go completely blank and let it tell me what to do. "Show me Ava," I commanded. When I opened my eyes, I saw that there was a sort of hologram projecting from the pearl. It was a small circular window that showed me whatever it was I wished to see. Ava was sitting at her throne discussing something with one of her creepy minion eels. I wasn't interested in hearing the conversation or seeing anymore of her. "Show me Aunt Morgan." As quickly as the image of Ava faded, the image of my Aunt Morgan appeared. She was at the surface, sprawled out on a giant rock basking in the sunshine. She looked so magnificent. Her beautiful long hair was fanned out behind her, and her skin was glistening. She looked like she had just taken a bath in fairy dust. She had given up so many of her own years for me. I wish I had spent more time learning from her. She had such control and restraint. It was if she wasn't cursed as we were. She tried to teach me to do the same, but looking back now, I realize that I wasn't interested. I studied her beauty and grace in my magic window and felt admiration, along with a bit of jealously at the same time. "Close," I commanded. The image faded, and my pearl was just a pearl once again.

There was one person I needed to see. My pulse quickened, and my stomach ached a bit with nervousness. I reached for my pearl and closed my eyes. "Show me Lee," I said in a whisper. The light projected from the pearl, and the image in my small window began to appear. There he was. There was my Lee. He was in the small book store on the island. He was sitting at a table surrounded by piles of books that seemed to reach beyond his own height. His dark eyes were intensely studying the words he was reading. Every few seconds he would bring one of his hands to his forehead and brush away the strands of dark hair that fell over his eyes. His eyes were moving back and forth so quickly across the pages he was reading I wondered what it was that fascinated him so. That was when I could clearly make out the title of the book atop of one of his tall towers. I brought my hand to my chest as I read the words, "Mermaids Among Men".

"Close," I commanded. There were so many thoughts swimming around one another in my mind, I couldn't catch up with them. I couldn't think, I couldn't begin to process what to do with this, and I certainly couldn't tell anyone. Less than a second later I was swimming as quickly and desperately as I ever had. I had to get to Lee, and I had to get there as quickly as possible.

CHAPTER
Eleven

IN THE TIME IT TOOK ME TO SWIM back to Gray Mist I must have examined every possible scenario I could imagine in my mind. I had so many questions. *How could Lee have possibly found out? Did he know I was a mermaid? Is he in danger? Could Adrian have told him?* I needed answers. It had taken a few days to get back to Gray Mist Island from Ava's lair. There was still time before I had to start worrying about the moon and my curse. A reunion with a not so old flame that began with murdering another guy after seducing him was probably not the brightest note to begin on. There was still no guarantee that I could be good; I wasn't taking any chances. I was taking enough of a risk simply by coming back here. This was a bad idea - I knew it. It was almost as if I was being physically pulled away, and swimming against the current to get here. That had to be the reason it took longer to get here than it ever had before.

When I finally reached the surface, I didn't get out. I stayed right where I was, with my head only inches above the water. It was night time; the air was crisp and cool. The smell of the surf and sand was a welcomed gift to my senses. The wind was gentle, and I took in all of the sounds of the waves crashing against the shore. I let myself relax for a moment, and then told myself it was time to find Lee. I had no idea what I was going to say or do when I found him, but I knew I had to make sure he was safe.

I swam a little closer to shore and hid behind a few large rocks. There was a couple enjoying one another by a fire they had made on the beach not far from where I was. They were tangled together and breathing heavily between kisses. I slowly swam toward them. My tail glided and swished from side to side gently behind me as I gracefully swam closer. I lifted myself to the shore with my arms, and waited a moment for my legs to form on the sand. I slowly stood up and walked over to them. The cool air tickled my bare skin. There was no one else on the beach for miles. I stood over them completely naked, then knelt to get the girl's sundress that was laying on the sand next to them. She was only in her bra and panties. She opened her eyes just long enough to see me, and let out a scream. The guy quickly jumped to his feet.

"What the fu…." he started to say. Before he had the chance to finish his sentence I had my hand over his mouth. My eyes commanded him to sit next to the girl. He did. They both looked at me with wide and worried eyes. The girl's chin was quivering, and the guy had both his arms locked protectively around her. The affection and love they had for one another was very apparent. I pulled the girls dress over my head, ran my fingers through my hair to comb out some of the tangles, and sat down in front of them.

"What do you want?" the girl cried. "Shhh," I said and put my hand on her arm.

I looked her into her eyes and said, "You never saw me. You have no idea what happened to your dress, and there is nothing to be afraid of." Then I looked at the guy, put a hand on his arm, and did the same. I stood up and walked along the beach wondering why humans were so easy to manipulate with magic. It wasn't the same with mermaids. As I walked away from the ocean I turned my head back to check on the couple. They had already forgotten all about me, their bodies were tangled together once again - they looked completely free and lost in one another. It made me think of Lee and the brief time I spent pretending I could actually have a small taste of that kind of life with him.

The soft crunch of the sand felt good under my feet and between my toes. I missed having legs and feeling my feet when I was in the water. These legs could walk for miles and miles without ever wanting to stop or rest. It seemed to only take minutes to be back on the somewhat more populated part of the island. I immediately knew that I didn't want to go anywhere near the hotel. Seeing Adrian would be too much, and the memories of Molly would be a distraction. I could not risk anyone else getting hurt because of me. The island seemed quieter and more abandoned than it normally was. I could hear every branch of every tree bending and moving with every soft breeze that flowed in. There was no traffic, no people passing by, and absolutely no noise. The crickets were chirping, the grass was gently swaying, and the frogs were croaking their songs together off in the distance. The street I was on led to a short path that led to another path along one of the lagoons. The peacefulness and calming sensation of the sounds seemed to be calling me towards the lagoon. As I walked along I admired the bats swooping down above the lagoon looking for their evening meal of insects. Bats were fascinating creatures. Their hunting abilities were unmatched, and they had a certain mystery about them I'd always admired. They were predators of the night. I envied their freedom - I envied the freedom of many animals. I watched them flying across the surface of the lagoon for another couple of minutes before bringing my hand to my necklace. I held the pearl in my hand and whispered, "Show me Lee."

There he was. The image of Lee was as clear as the waters of the Maldives Islands on the Indian Ocean. He was right where I knew he would be. He sat with his back propped against the giant Oak tree looking out into the ocean. His dark hair was messy and carelessly laying over his forehead. His eyes were dark with intensity, and a little sad at the same time. He looked beautiful. His white tee shirt fit well enough to just outline his strong shoulders. He wore a pair of tan colored cargo shorts and pair of flip flops. Lee was so effortlessly beautiful. There was a coolness and a quiet sensuality that he projected without even knowing it. Looking at him now I wondered how I ever thought I could honestly stay away from him. There was something about him that I needed. It was beyond desire, lust, or love; it was a basic primal need I had for him. I let my pearl necklace fall to my chest and headed to him, to my beautiful Lee.

The night wind blew my hair up behind me as I ran towards Lee. The wind zipped past my cheeks, and I could taste the salt in the air. The faster I approached the beach and the Oak tree, the louder the crashing of the waves against the shore became. Every crash was another warning, "Stop, come to the water, do not expose yourself, dive in before you have gone too far."

I ignored every warning. I understood with perfect clarity how foolish this was. The problem was, I didn't have a choice. I never had a choice when it came to Lee. You hear humans say all the time that they always have a choice. They may not have good choices, but they have choices. That logic doesn't work the same with hybrids, or mermaids for that matter. When your natural instincts kick in there is no fighting it. You will lose every single time. It's like the moon's power over the tides. It's a force of nature that won't be ignored or waited for. Perhaps in some ways we were no more civilized than animals in the wild. I had to go to him.

The impressive tree stood before me. Its enormous branches were as twisted and turned as my mind was at this moment. The tree was the only thing standing between Lee and I, and I knew it didn't want me anywhere near him - nothing in nature wanted me anywhere near him right now. I didn't care. I was strong enough to do this, and this is what I was going to do. That was the only thought in my mind as I slowly walked toward him. Every step I took was one step closer to the unknown. The slower I walked, the faster my heart beat. For all I knew he could try to kill me. I had absolutely no idea what I was walking into. I paused when I reached the tree. I took a deep breath, and walked around the wide trunk until I was standing right next to where he was sitting.

He quickly jumped to his feet as if he had just seen a ghost. Once on his feet he looked me over, and slowly took a few steps back. His eyes were wide, his eyebrows were raised, and his lips were slightly parted. His chest rose and fell as his breath quickened. I took a step towards him, and put a hand in the air. He took another step back.

"Okay," I said. "Okay. I will stay right where I am." I put my hand down and stopped walking.

He narrowed his eyes.

"I know," he said.

I nodded my head.

"I figured." I looked down at the sand and then off toward the ocean. "How do you know?"

"You don't get to ask me questions, Kai." He was angry. I could feel his anger now, and it was strong. He ran his fingers through his hair, "What the hell?" he yelled. He stood there looking at me wincing. He shook his head back and forth, paced a few steps, then turned back around to look at me again.

"I'm sorry," I whispered. There were tears in my eyes now.

"You're sorry? You're sorry? Oh, that's great, she's sorry. That makes everything better doesn't it?"

"I need to know that you aren't going to do anything with this information."

"That is what you are worried about?" That is all you have to say to me? Can't you just do your mermaid magic and force me to forget you anyway?"

"No. That is not all I am worried about, and yes, I could do that, but I don't want to." I took a step closer to him; he didn't back away this time. "I need to know that you are safe."

"I'm not going to expose you, Kai. Everyone would think I was crazier than they probably already do anyway. Besides, I promised Adrian I wouldn't." He was still angry.

Adrian had told him, I should have figured that out.

I took one last look at him, and did everything I could not to fall to his feet in tears begging for his forgiveness. I bit my lower lip, managed to hold back the rest of my tears, and started to walk away. He didn't want me. What did I expect? He must think I was some kind of freak. I ran. I ran as fast as I could to the water, ripped off my dress, and dove in. Just as my head went under I heard him calling me from afar.

"Kai! Kai! Wait, please wait!"

I stopped dead in my tracks, mid-stroke, and let myself come back to the surface. When my head was above water I saw him. He didn't look as appalled or as in shock as I thought he would. He walked closer to the water. We were still at least 15 feet away from one another. He threw off his shoes, and walked until he was about knee deep in the water. I stayed right where I was.

"I need to ask you something," he said. His tone was softer now. "Was I just another human to toy with? Were you going to use me, then kill me?

I shook my head back and forth and started crying again.

"No."

"Were you ever planning on it, even in the beginning?" He asked.

"No. I don't know. I don't think so. I saw you around, and there was something about you. There was just something that pulled me closer to you. I saw you here one night, and I knew I could never hurt you. You know the rest of it." I wiped the tears from my eyes. "I'm so sorry, Lee. I don't know what else to say."

"Yeah…I'm sorry too. I thought you were my forever. I loved you, Kai."

"I guess that was when you thought I was just a girl," I smiled.

"Yeah. Yeah, I guess so," he said. "I don't know. I see you now, and part of me still wants you, still loves you. Look at you. How could I not? But, how could it ever be? And even if it could, how could I ever trust that you won't go all psycho killer mermaid on me?"

"Why aren't you more afraid or I don't know, impressed? It's not every day your ex-girlfriend shows up with a tail, right?"

He smiled, and shook his head.

"Can we sit for a while, and I'll tell you?"

"I can't like this, not here."

He walked back to the sand, and picked up my dress.

"Come back up here then," he said.

"Okay." I swam closer to the shore, watching him watching me. His eyes were narrowed, and he looked at me exactly as he did before. Whatever was between us was still there. I felt it, and I could feel him now too. I sat at the shore and let my tail transform back into legs. He watched it happen with wide eyes. Now he looked impressed, and a little freaked out.

"Wow," he whispered.

He held my dress out for me to take, and turned his head as I threw it on over my head.

We started walking back to the tree. He reached for my hand. As our fingers clasped and locked together I felt tiny little sparks of electricity flickering around in my hand. He walked in silence for a few seconds, then he started talking again.

"After you left, I was a mess. I packed up everything and hit the road looking for you for a solid week. When I realized I had no idea where to look anymore, I came back to the Island."

His voice was deep and smooth. It was so soothing. I listened without interrupting.

"Adrian has always been good to me. I look up to him, and sometimes talk through things with him. I went to the hotel one day hoping to find some trace of you. It was tough being there after Molly, but I couldn't just let you go like that."

When he said Molly's name, I tensed up. *Poor Molly. That was all my fault.* Lee must have sensed what I was feeling.

"I know you didn't kill Molly, Kai. I know what you have done, but I don't think that is really what you are." My heart felt full again.

"Do you mean that?" I asked.

He shifted his weight a little from side to side.

"Yeah…yeah I do." We sat down in front of the tree together. "Anyway, I told Adrian how upset I was. I was in a pretty dark place. I felt like things couldn't get any worse, and I was lost. I was completely lost." He sighed, "That's when he told me he was your father, and he told me about you."

Adrian knew he was my father, and said nothing to me about it?

"You accepted it to be true? You had to have been in complete disbelief," I said.

"I was. That's when he proved it to me. That's why I was not in complete shock when I saw you jump in the water. You're not the first mermaid I've seen, Kai."

I should have been surprised, but I wasn't. It seemed that nothing should surprise me anymore. I sat there staring at him, wondering if he could see the complete lack of surprise on my face. There was a small part of me that was a little let down that I wasn't the first mermaid he had ever seen.

So much for that grand gesture.

He was sitting there waiting for some sort of reaction from me. I gave him nothing. His eyes narrowed as if he couldn't accept that I wasn't completely freaking out right now. I was looking at him wondering if I could accept that he wasn't completely freaking out right now. This was certainly an interesting position that we were in. I felt our thoughts weaving and tangling around one another into a beautiful confused mess. He finally spoke first, "So…uh…don't you have a million questions for me?"

I looked down at my feet, and then back up at him.

"I suppose not. I would imagine if you wanted me to know something you would tell me." I turned so that my entire body was facing his, "Why did you call me back, Lee? Why are we sitting here?"

"I," he sighed, "I don't know. All I've been thinking about all this time is what I would say to you when the day came that I finally found you, and now we are here I don't know where to begin." He winced, then ran his long fingers through his beautiful careless hair. "I know part of me is angry as hell at you for making me feel what I feel for you. Part of me wishes I could erase you from my heart and my soul, but I know it's nothing that I'd ever do. I like having you there, having you here," he put his hand over his heart. I was having trouble holding back my tears. My poor Lee. He was so vulnerable, and needed so much to be loved and understood. His hand found mine, and he brought it to the place it rested a moment ago on his chest. "I still feel you right here," he said. My hand was still on his chest. Without a second of hesitation my hand glided up his chest and around the back of his neck. My fingers found his hair, our mouths were less than an inch apart. His warm breath on my lips awoken every bit of my body. My skin was singing with excitement, my body began literally aching for him to touch me. We were caught in that moment that comes right before the climbing anticipation of who is going to move in first. I wanted it to be him.

Kiss me. Kiss me. Kiss me, was all I could think.

After what seemed like forever, he wrapped his arms around my waist and kissed me. And he was really kissing me. His lips were soft and full. He kissed me softly again and again before our lips slightly parted so that our tongues could meet. These were the best kisses ever. We were both in tears of pure joy as we kissed one another with more passion than we ever had before. Every kiss I was telling him how much I loved him. He ran his hands up and down my back and my arms. His hands felt so good. I wanted them to cover every inch of me. They quickly found their way to my breasts where he gently grabbed them, and traced my nipples with his fingers. Now I wanted him, really wanted him. I ran my hands through his hair, and pulled a little to let him know how badly I needed him. His hands moved inside of my dress, he was touching my bare breasts. I softly moaned, and we both started breathing heavily. My stomach cramped up in knots of passion and desire. Our kisses became more and more like we were grasping on to one another as if our lives depended on it. I slowly slid my hand over his chest, and then down his pants. He let out a cry of passion. I bit my lip, and smiled at him. Our eyes locked as I unzipped his pants. He grabbed me firmly by my hips then lifted me on top of him so I was straddling him. Our eyes remained locked on one another as he gently slid inside of me and we made love. We rocked back and forth in rhythm with the crashing waves. I let my dress fall around my waist so I could show him my bare breasts in the moonlight. I felt waves of ecstasy rising and falling inside of me with every move we made. When it was over we both fell back on the ground together. He held on to me like he was never going to let me go. I snuggled up to him so that we fit together like a perfect puzzle. He kissed my forehead, and stroked my hair a few times.

"Be with me, Kai," he whispered. "I'll do anything. Just be with me."

I closed my eyes and took a deep breath.

"I love you, Lee."

"And I love you."

That was all we said. We didn't talk about his mermaid sightings or my past. We didn't talk about Adrian or what was going to happen next. We didn't talk for hours. We just lied in one another's arms and got lost together under the stars.

It was nearly sunrise. The night had gotten away from us. We were still lying in one another's arms. I turned my head to look up at him, and saw that he was sleeping peacefully. He had a slight smile on his face that made him appear angelic somehow. I ran my fingers through his messy hair and let myself take this moment in one last time. There was so much we hadn't talked about; there was so much more to say to one another. I nuzzled my nose in the nook of his neck, kissed him softly on the forehead, and wriggled my way out of his embrace without disturbing him. I got up and ran as fast as I could to the water. It was only seconds before I was diving in, and swimming as fast as I could to say goodbye to the sea once and for all. I wanted to be with Lee. He was worth risking everything, losing everything, and I knew I would have no regrets. I swam so quickly everything around me was a blur - all I could see was the ripples in the water ahead of me. It was time for me to embrace my soul, even if it meant having to go mad. I knew it was the only way to be with him without risking his life. He was worth it.

CHAPTER

THE WATER CARESSED EVERY INCH of my skin as I swam deeper into
the darkness of her embrace. It was warm, welcoming, and comforting. If only those feelings were not so quickly replaced with
feelings of uncertainty and betrayal. If I let myself love the water,
I felt as if I was somehow betraying Lee. When I was completely
consumed in Lee, I felt as if I were betraying the water. I was torn
between two worlds.

My necklace felt cool against my chest; I had forgotten all
about it for a few minutes. The coolness took me by surprise. My
chest began to tighten, I felt short of breath. My necklace was
warning me somehow. I stopped swimming, brought my hand to
my chest, and rubbed my pearl between my thumb and index finger. My eyes opened wider as I saw what it was trying to show me.

I saw Liana with Ava. I could only see brief snapshots, but it
was enough to see what was going on. Liana was obviously working for my mother. Why had I not considered that before? I saw
the two of them plotting and planning. I saw Ava give Liana a
mixture of mermaid blood and something else. I intuitively knew
it was meant for Lee. It was Liana that had exposed Lee to our
kind. There was a flash of Liana swimming to shore to allow Lee
to see her. He looked terrified. She nearly snatched him up, but

Adrian came running after him. The moment Liana saw Adrian it looked like she was literally pulled back under the water by a force much more powerful than she was. She was violently snatched under. Had she been mortal, she would have drowned and died. I'd be willing to bet Ava had something to do with that. I wasn't sure if she had some sort of protection spell on my father or if she was watching and waiting to make her move, but I knew this was all her doing. She is a great many things, but I completely believed that she loved Adrian. I could feel it. The next images I saw were of Lee and Adrian. They were having what looked like an impossible conversation. Everything was beginning to come together now. If only I knew what was happening, and why Liana was going to give Lee mermaid blood. I didn't see Liam in any of these warnings. I hoped he was not a part of any of this. I genuinely believed he and I connected when we spent time together. It would be nice to know I had one friend down here. Perhaps none of us could be trusted after all. One thing was certain; I needed to find Liam. I had to at least find out if I could trust him; I had to know. "Show me Liam," I commanded. He wasn't far from here. I could sense that much. I couldn't tell exactly where he was, but I knew my pearl would guide me. He was swimming in open water. There was no one else within miles of him. This was the perfect time to catch him, and get to the bottom of Liana's involvement with Ava.

As I pushed through the water ahead of me I could sense I was getting closer to him. There was something genuinely believable about Liam. When he and I spoke, and swam together I felt like we understood one another somehow. Liam was a merman; I understood enough about our kind to approach with caution. Cursed or not, there were still good sea dwellers and bad. The world beneath the surface of land was another world all together, but some of the same basic principles and rules still applied to its inhabitants. Anger, frustration, and confusion consumed me. He would not be capable of lying to me, his thoughts would be easy enough to read. My powers were heightened since I was given my immortality. There was no hiding anything from me. He was close.

He was in front of me. Liam looked troubled. His eyes didn't sparkle the way they had when I first met him. It appeared as though dark clouds were slowly moving over his normally stunning eyes. He swam closer to me until we were merely arm length apart from one another. He began speaking before I could read his thoughts. Whatever he was going to tell me was true, that much I knew already.

"Kai. I thought our paths would cross again."

"Hello, Liam. Where is Lia..." He interrupted me. His normal almost regal appearance was replaced with a look of disarray. His face appeared tired looking. I could read the worry in his eyes.

"I knew nothing of her involvement with Ava. I need you to believe me."

I nodded. My chest began to tighten, but I remained calm and let him explain.

"Okay," I said.

There was an expression of hurt that covered his entire face. He wore it beautifully. I felt hurt for him, as I became more and more in sync with his emotions and feelings.

"Liana is gone. I'm not sure she will return."

I was only now realizing Liana was Liam's sister.

Why hadn't I picked up on that before?

Sometimes we are so consumed by ourselves, we can't see what is right in front of us. There is a saying about being blinded by love; I think we are blinded by ourselves. We are blinded to everything around us when we are caught up in our own tangled scenarios.

"She thought earning Ava's trust would position her better somehow,"

"What does that mean?"

"I'm not entirely certain."

I was doing everything in my power to stay cool and collected. His vagueness was not making it easy.

"Liam, I know you don't have anything to do with whatever it is that is happening right now. I can read your thoughts. You have to let me know what is going on."

He seemed a bit more comfortable now. He let his shoulders relax, and took a deep breath. He looked at me, and then quickly shifted his eyes downward.

"Liana is working with Ava. The details are uncertain." Liam was telling the truth. He didn't know anything more. He brought his hands to his chest and winced, "I suspect it has something to do with you."

"I suspect your suspicions are correct." I sighed and shook my head. Endless possibilities were swimming through my mind. Ava drank darkness and pain like fine wine. What I couldn't understand was how Liana fit into all of this.

Was it my power she wanted? Did she wish to rule by Ava's side?

I'd happily bestow that honor upon her at this point. Liam looked at me again, his eyes still full of worry. He swam closer to me, then reached for my hands.

"Kai, I don't want to see you hurt. I hope that my sister is not a part of something diabolical. She thirsts for power and acceptance in a way I simply cannot begin to understand." I squeezed his hands, then let them go.

"I know you love your sister, Liam. My wish is not to make you choose between your love for her and something else." He knew what I meant. There was no reason to say more.

"I wonder if my Aunt knows about any of this," I said.

Liam raised his eyebrows, "Do you think that is possible?"

I shook my head, "No. I don't think so, but I wouldn't discount anything at this point. Every time I think I am closer to understanding something I find myself a bit more lost at sea." It was in that moment I felt Liam's affection for me. He truly was a friend. More and more I realized he might be the only actual friend I had in this world or the other.

"I saw Ava and your sister conspiring. I think Liana exposed herself to Lee in an attempt to pull him under. I can't be certain, I only have brief images to work with. There was a mixture with mermaid blood and something else…" My voice trailed off. "Do you think they are trying to kill him?"

"Kai, I wish I had the answers for you. I wish I had even one answer for you."

I managed to find a soft smile to give him. "I guess I need to go directly to the source if I want to get answers," I said.

"Are you going to try to regain complete attachment to your soul?" He asked.

"Yes. You don't have to say more, I can hear the disapproval in your thoughts."

"Do you know what that will mean for you, what it could mean for you?" His concern was practically written in the sand on the bottom of the ocean floor. He was afraid for me.

"I do. Nothing is perfect, right?" My shallow attempt to put his mind at ease was failing miserably. He didn't respond. He simply looked at me knowing there was nothing he could say to sway my opinion or change my mind. I didn't have time to discuss this. The truth was I didn't know what this meant. His thoughts warned me to consider the risks I'd be taking. His heart was full of pity and concern because all he saw was an existence of pain and torment for me. "Thank you for your help, Liam. I appreciate you. I need to get to Ava now more than ever." Instinctively I swam closer in to embrace him. His arms welcomed my gesture, and he squeezed me tightly. We lingered in front of one another for a moment, it was a moment away from being awkward. I flipped my tail and turned to swim away. I looked over my shoulder, "I'll see you soon. I promise." He smiled as convincingly as he could, trying to hide his disapproval. I couldn't think about what that meant right now. The water pushed me along, with every movement I was an instant closer to getting answers. Perhaps I was even closer to my soul. I'd swim for days if that is what it took. Luckily, it wouldn't take long at all.

The pearl around my neck guided me closer to Ava. She and Liana were together, thick as thieves.

What was it they were after?

Fortunately, they were in her lair, which was truly more of an underwater kingdom. Finding her grounds was easier now that I'd been there a few times. Everything was still. The water was dark, but calm. The beautiful guards all stood fierce with their spears and austere expressions. I expected them to protest or try to stop me from entering, but none of them did. They all allowed me to swim past and through the entrance to see my mother. I swam directly to where she sat arrogantly on her throne. Liana was positioned directly in front of her, her tail was swaying slowly back and forth. Liana's hands were crossed over her chest. They were arguing. Silence fell over both of them as I approached. Liana turned her head to look at me as I swam closer to the two of them. Her expression was vacant of any emotion. I didn't have to ask. I didn't have to say anything. I could hear Liana's thoughts as clear as chimes dancing in the breeze. My soul. They were trying to steal my soul.

CHAPTER
Thirteen

I PLUNGED TOWARDS LIANA at full force. My movements were so fast she didn't have time to defend herself. My nails slipped into her flesh like a knife slicing through warm butter. Her eyes were full of fear. My eyes must have looked mad with rage. I pushed her with the water into the side of Ava's throne. She shrieked out in pain. Once I had her pinned I loosened my grip on her. I was much stronger than she was - another perk of being the Sea Witch's daughter I guess. Her thoughts were begging and pleading for me not to hurt her.

"If I could kill you, you would already be dead," I whispered to her. Our faces were only inches apart. I wanted to claw her beautiful eyes out, and feed them to the sea serpents. Before I could say anything else, Ava interrupted.

"Enough, Kai. You are going to have her skin under your nails for days if you don't let go of her." Liana looked gratefully at Ava for what she hoped for would be a break in my attack on her. I let her go, pushing her with full force away from me. Then I snapped my head around to look at Ava. I was fueled full of rage.

"Were you planning on sharing my soul with her? You can't seem to stop proving to me over and over what a monster you are." Ava smiled coldly, shook her head back and forth a few times, and

laughed. Her laughter chimed as it always did. I was truly beginning to hate the sound of her laughter. I was truly beginning to
hate the mere sight of her.

"Of course, I was not going to share your soul with anyone.
Don't be insolent." Ava raised one perfectly arched eyebrow then
blinked slowly a few times as if for dramatic effect, "I am trying
to help you! Why are you so unwilling to see that? Liana is serving
me." She changed her tone to almost a whisper, "You would do
well to remember that every creature in these waters serve me." I
hadn't forgotten. How could I?

Asking Ava why she wanted my soul was foolish. I knew exactly
what she was trying to accomplish; she wanted me to embrace my
darkness. She also knew that the sole purpose of this most recent
trip under water was to tell her once and for all that I was choosing
Lee. She looked over at Liana, waved a hand, and dismissed her.
Liana smiled smugly at me as she swam away. She was the least of
my concern. Ava summoned her, and she responded. I knew now
there was nothing more to her involvement than that. There was
not much I could do to Liana even if I wanted to harm her. She was
immortal, and more importantly if I caused her any harm I knew
it would hurt Liam. I could feel it when I looked at him. Besides,
almost any mermaid under the sea would dive at the chance to get
in good with the all-powerful Ava. It sickened me. Any negotiations
with Ava were officially off the table. She destroyed any chance of
salvaging any sort of relationship with me when she involved Lee.
I knew she meant him harm. She would have forced Liana to do
her dirty work, but it was her hand in control - as it always was. She
stared at me with cold eyes listening in on every thought running
through my mind. I didn't care. I wasn't afraid of her anymore. She
needed me much more than I needed her.

I looked at her every bit as determined as she was. I crossed my arms across my chest and narrowed my eyes to glare at her.

"I want every bit of my soul attached to my body."

"It is never going to happen, Kai," she winced.

"I know you have the power to do this," I cried.

"Of course I do," she said.

There was something about her tone, or perhaps it was the look in her eyes that gave it away. In that instant I knew exactly how possible it was to have my soul restored. I gasped aloud, and brought my hands to my mouth. My chest tightened, and my heart felt as if it could beat straight through my chest.

"All this time," I whispered. "All this time." I backed away from her a bit; maybe I wanted to get a full frame view of this moment. For a moment, it felt like I was watching someone else's life play out in front of my eyes. "This is why you were tying so desperately to steal my soul and hide it." Ava said nothing. She was expressionless. For a few minutes, we were both perfectly still, we were facing one another in complete silence. It was so silent even the noise from the ripples in the water seemed amplified. Had another sea creature swam past us at this moment, it would have sounded like a thousand waves crashing at once. Ava was the one to break the silence between us.

"So there it is. Do what you will. I can no longer try to protect you from yourself."

"Is that what you were doing with the mermaid blood and Lee? Were you trying to protect from me from myself?"

"The blood would not have harmed him. I made sure of that. It simply would have erased all of his memories of you. He would have remembered nothing, and we all would have been safer for it," she said.

"Your blood can turn into almost any mystical charm or incantation you desire. You could restore my soul with one drop of your blood," I whispered. Ava nodded and turned from me. She slowly turned back around to face me. Her expression was somber now.

"And now you have finally realized your blood holds the same power," she replied. "You are every bit as powerful as I am, perhaps you will become more powerful in time. I know you don't believe me, and I know you do not want to accept this, but I truly am trying to save you." She brought her right hand to her chest, and gently tapped over where her heart is. "I beg you, don't do this," she said.

It was too late. I knew what I needed to do to become one with my soul without ever losing it to the moon again. My blood was the key. It was so simple. The understanding of this hit me all at once. Something happened when Ava and I locked eyes; I just knew. I knew it. What happened next was nothing I could have foreseen, not even with my powers of vision. Ava reached out and put her hand on my shoulder and nodded. Then she slowly pulled her hand from my shoulder, flipped her hand over so that her wrist was face up, and brought it to my lips.

"Go ahead, Kai. Drink."

Our eyes locked. She meant it. Those four words were the most important words I would ever hear.

"Go ahead, Kai. Drink."

I wrapped my fingers around her forearm, brought my lips to her wrist, closed my eyes, and sunk my teeth into her flesh. Her blood flowed into my mouth as easily as if I were drinking wine - dark, silky, warm red wine. As her blood trickled over my tongue and down my throat I felt a kind of warmth that can only be described as nurturing. This was completely different than feeding from a human. This was calming. This was peaceful. I fed on her blood like an infant nursing from its mother. I instinctively knew when I had consumed enough, and quickly pulled myself from her. I felt nothing other than peaceful, which was the exact opposite of what I expected to feel. Ava looked down at her wrist, which healed itself in less than a second, then looked back at me. She placed her hand on my cheek as she often did, and blinked very slowly a few times.

"So it is complete. Your soul is all yours once again. The moon, the old ones, and the water have no claim to it. You are now the center of your own universe."

I pressed my lips together, and blinked a few times. Part of my mind was still metabolizing what just happened.

"What happens now? Will it be painful? Will I feel any different?" I said almost all at once. Ava took her place at her throne. She looked so powerful and incredibly royal sitting there as she ran one hand along the top of her black shimmering tail.

"Physically you won't feel any different. It's not as if you haven't felt the pull of your soul occasionally up until this point. That remorse and guilt is what got you here to begin with. The difference is, you no longer have those days to give in completely to your darkness. You no longer have those times to throw all of that guilt into the sea. In time, every ounce of guilt and remorse will come flooding back to you. Make no mistake, you will drown in it. It may not happen tomorrow; it may not happen in two months' time, but it will happen. When it happens, it will be all at once." Aunt Morgan's face flashed before my eyes.

"What about...." She stopped me before I completed my thought.

"No, Morgan cannot heal you. Her power doesn't work that way." She sighed, "I suppose you will be going to the surface now to find your human?"

"Yes," I said with a little more arrogance than I had intended. Ava had just given me her own blood to give me what I wanted.

My tone softened, "I'm very strong. This won't destroy me," I said.

"I believe that you believe that. I hope you are correct, but I don't have to remind you of the countless lives you have taken do I? How much pleasure have you taken in other people's pain on that very same surface you are so eager to return to? Make no mistake, my desire is not to see you lose yourself in madness. You are my daughter, and you will always have a place here beside me. That said, this is not what I wanted for you," she said shaking her head. "Yes, I attempted to steal your soul and I would do it again if I thought it would change anything. I know now that it won't."

There was nothing she was telling me I hadn't heard before. Part of me knew she might be right. It was a chance I was willing to take to be with him. I had to. I think my soul must have caught on fire the moment our eyes met. I never really had a choice.

"I know you don't approve, and I'm not sure where this leaves us. When I arrived here I was certain I'd hate you forever. I appreciate what you have done for me."

"Kai," she called.

"Yes?"

"There is something else you should know. If it should come to you going mad with guilt, I can pull your soul from you once again. If it comes to that, you will never regain it again; it will be lost to you forever. You need to know this." Her eyes told me she was telling the truth. Her soft and sorrowful expression that consumed her impossibly beautiful face told me she was terribly worried for me.

"Please be careful above. I'm unable to help you as long as you are on land." She seemed genuinely sad to be losing me again for what seemed like the hundredth time. I couldn't help but wonder if my decision might be different if she hadn't abandoned me to begin with. She claims she did what was best for me - she claims she did what she had to do to because she loved me. If all of that were true, why couldn't I wrap my head around the idea of a child growing up without parents ever being the better decision? Abandonment is one of the worst things a child can experience. It goes on and on for years and years. Growing up without a mother or a father impacts our ability to trust, it makes relationships incredibly difficult for us, and it almost certainly will take us much longer to learn how to love ourselves - let alone growing up without a mother or a father. No one is asked to be born, and we certainly don't want to be left alone without parents after being put here. We go on for years wondering what it might be like to have a Mom and a Dad. Birthdays are hard, holidays are painful, and we never quite fit in anywhere. No, I couldn't believe for an instant that leaving your child behind was ever the best thing. I'd never believe it. I gave her one last long look, nodded my head to express I understood what she was telling me, and swam away from her once again.

Excitement, fear, and nervousness consumed all of my thoughts. Knowing my soul was entirely mine once again brought me indescribable happiness. Never again would I feel myself separating from it, never again would I feel myself drawn to the seductive violence I embraced for so long. I could finally be me again, or at least figure out exactly who that was. Perhaps I could finally learn to love myself. With every turn I made under the water I felt a little more darkness lift away from me. With every swoosh of my tail the closer I knew I was to happiness above the surface; I was closer to Lee.

Time moved differently under the water. If I had been trying to keep track of the time as I made my way through the waves, I lost it. The only thing I could feel was the desire to feel my feet again. I couldn't wait to feel my toes in the sand, the relief and pleasure of stretching the muscles in my long human legs, and to feel my hips sway back and forth as I moved. Being human never seemed so wonderful until now. Of course, I'd never really be human. The water would still call to me every full moon and I would swim, but the thirst for human life would be gone. The light inside of me would finally be free to shine. Lee's beautiful face was all I could see. Lee's eyes, Lee's mouth, Lee's hair falling over his forehead. He polluted my thoughts in the best possible way. I swam on and on thinking of nothing but him, until I saw Liam's face flash across my thoughts. "Liam," I said aloud. He needed to know I hadn't harmed Liana, and he needed to know I was safe. I stopped swimming, reached for my pearl, held it between my fingers, and commanded it to show me where Liam was.

"You don't need to track me down, Kai. I'd never hide from you," said a voice hidden behind a school of yellow tailed fish swimming by. It was Liam. I let my pearl fall back against my chest. It was curious that I hadn't heard his thoughts or sensed him nearby as I was swimming. I guess I was so consumed in everything else I closed off part of my mind without realizing it. The sound of his voice was nice. Once the school passed by I could see him. He was barley moving, waiting for me to approach him. We both smiled and laughed.

"Who said I thought you were hiding from me?"

"I've come to expect you not to trust any of us down here," he said slowly. I had to admit I loved everything about the way Liam presented himself. Everything about him radiated magic, confidence, and strength. He was completely opposite of Lee, and of course there was the human verses being a merman thing going on.

"I trust you. You know that."

"I hope so, Kai."

"Are you going to try to stop me?"

"Take on the daughter of the most powerful creature in the sea? I wouldn't dare. There is the other issue of my genuine hope for you to find peace and happiness." His eyes were full of honesty, and affection. He moved closer to embrace me. His arms were God like, I felt very fragile in his embrace. It was nice. Our tails entwined, we held on to one another for a couple of minutes before I let go. I could hear his thoughts asking me if there was anything he could say or do to keep me here.

"Kai, you could keep your soul and stay under the water. You know that, don't you?"

"I do." "But…." my voice trailed off.

"I know. Do what you must. Please be careful up there. If the madness begins to take over, promise me you will come find me. The thought of you risking exposure, and what the repercussions of that may be is agony. Please promise me."

"I promise." I hugged him again, stroked his hair, and kissed him on the cheek. I turned to swim away, and he reached for my hand.

"Kai, your human may not be the only one to have you in their life. I'd happily let you invade my immortality. You are such a perfect creature. I would be honored to spend a thousand years reminding you of that every moment of every day. I understand you. I understand what you are with perfect clarity and I want every bit of you." He brought his other hand to the small of my back. His expression was intense, he was gorgeous. His face was inches away from mine now. I'd never been this close to one of my kind before. I'd only ever kissed and touched human men. He let go of my hand so that both his hands were around my waist now. His lips softly touched mine. He gently put both lips on just my bottom lip, then pressed his entire mouth against mine. Waves of electricity, excitement, and pure pleasure washed over me. It was like nothing I'd ever felt before. My head was spinning, the water moved quickly around us creating a whirlpool effect. My fingers were tingling, my body was buzzing, my soul was singing; the intensity of this was like nothing else I'd ever known existed. This was magical. We were kissing more passionately, every time his tongue touched mine I thought I'd pass out from the overwhelming ecstasy. I was elated to be in his strong embrace. Muscles were contracting in my body that I didn't even know I had. My body was trembling, I could have died completely happy in this moment. He felt so good. I had to pull away before I let things go too far.

"I'm sorry. I shouldn't have let that happen," I said trembling.

"Don't apologize." He brought a finger to my lips, and smiled. "I've needed to do that for some time now."

"I'm still going."

"I know you are. Perhaps now you will understand what it means to have something to come back to. You belong here, Kai. I won't stand in your way; I want you to find whatever it is you are looking for, but you belong here. I'll be here. I'd wait forever for you, and it just so happens that I have that much time." I smiled. Then I nodded, put my hand over my heart, and swam to Lee. I knew I had complicated feelings for Liam, I also knew that Lee was the one I wanted to be with again. He had given me a taste of happiness in a relationship, and I wanted more of it. As I swam away I realized I never told Liam anything of Liana. He didn't ask either. I'm sure she would make her way back to him soon enough, if she hadn't done so already. I shouldn't worry about any of that right now; I finally reached the island. It was finally time.

CHAPTER
Fourteen

ONCE I HAD MY FEET ON LAND, found clothing, and put myself together I began my search for Lee. My pearl could have led me straight to him, but I liked the idea of finding him simply because I sensed him. There was something romantic and whimsical about finding him that way. As I walked throughout the small town I saw familiar faces and a few new ones here and there. I didn't speak to anyone, I don't think anyone really recognized me anyway. There were only a few people on the entire island I'd ever bothered getting to know. It was much safer for me that way. Lost in my thoughts, all I could think of was reuniting with Lee. *Would we run into one another's arms? Which one of us would speak first? What would he say? What would I say?* Scenario after scenario played out in my mind. I imagined I'd find him sitting quietly reading a book, then I would sneak up quietly behind him and whisper, "I love you," in his ear. He would turn around so I could see his expression of pure joy when he laid eyes on me again. He kissed my face at least fifty times, threw his arms around me, and lifted me in the air like something out of romance novel or film. In another fantasy, I found him lying on the beach with his eyes closed and his hands folded behind his head. He would instinctively know I was near him and sit up quickly like something caused him to jump out of his sleep. He would take one look at me and shake his head in disbelief. "You came back to me," he would say. I would run right into his embrace and kiss him passionately until we were undressing one another and making love on the beach. I wish one of those scenarios, or one of the other dozens I had flickering through my thoughts had been our fate that day.

After circling the entire island for almost the third time I stopped walking. I felt nothing. There was nothing but vast emptiness all around me. He wasn't here. My thoughts quickly drifted to Adrian long enough to let me know that he was not anywhere on the island either. They were both gone. *Was this my punishment for all of the horrible things I've done? Was I destined to live out my immortality completely alone and unloved?* Perhaps that was exactly what I deserved. My heart felt heavy beneath my chest. My soul was crying out in pain. I was aching and feeling broken. This is what I deserved. My fingers finally found their way to my pearl. My heart began beating faster and faster as I demanded to see Lee.

There he was. He wasn't gone at all. Why I couldn't sense him was uncertain; why I didn't see him was uncertain, but he was close. He was sitting inside the book store chatting with Jeremy, the shop owner. "Why hadn't I thought to look in Seaside Stories," I wondered aloud. It was only a few minutes' walk from where I was standing near the beach. The idea of Lee being anything but elated to lay eyes on me again hadn't crossed my mind. The only thing that mattered was getting to him as quickly as I could. Everything else would fall right into place - it had to. I'd gone through so much to be with him. A life on land with Lee was the only thing I could see. The moon and the waves would pull me to the water once a month when I would swim, but I'd never hunt again. Living between two worlds was nothing new to me; I lived several years not truly belonging in one world or the other.

The land had never truly felt like it could be home for me until I fell in love with Lee. It was nothing more than hunting grounds for so many years. It had become my own personal playground for dark and deviant games, games I enjoyed and became almost consumed by. The water felt more like home to me, although I always came back up to the surface. I spent my entire life as a hybrid up to this point searching for something in one world or the other. Maybe now I could finally stop searching and start living.

The book store was only a few steps away now. The front door was propped open. I noticed a few new plants outside the front windows. The smell of the plants somehow seemed to make the store more inviting. Jeremy was walking to the back of the store with a pile of books in his arms. He didn't notice me walk in. Lee was sitting across the store at a small table. He was writing. He looked very engrossed in whatever it was he was writing. It made my heart happy to see him writing; he always talked about writing the way people talk about someone they love. There is no other way to explain it. I'd known a few writers in my travels. Writers loved to write. They are beautifully complicated human beings. Writers don't simply dig into the deepest darkest places in their minds and memories to pull inspiration, they exploit their own darkness, and they run wild with it. Writers are dishonest and honest all at the same time. They are narcissistic, imperious, and arrogant one moment then insecure, uncertain, and disconcerted the next. Lee was all of these things and I loved every bit of it. I started slowly walking toward him. I couldn't take my eyes off him. Silently I was willing him to look up at me. My hands were shaking; suddenly I had absolutely no idea what I was going to say to him. I didn't need to say anything. He stopped writing and raised his eyes to take me in.

"Kai," he whispered. He stood up and walked over to me.

"How are you.....here right now?" There was shock, confusion, and uncertainty written all over his beautiful face.

"Can we go somewhere to talk?"

"I...I guess so." There was nothing in his voice that led me to believe he was particularly happy to see me. This wasn't the reaction I hoped for, if I hoped for anything at all. I reminded myself to take a step back to appreciate how confusing and impossible this must be for him.

Lee and I walked out of the store and continued down the street in silence for a few minutes. This wasn't the way I imagined this moment at all. Lee walked with his hands in his pockets; it was almost like he wanted to keep them guarded and away from me. His eyes never really left the ground as we walked. He wasn't looking at me at all. My mind raced with thoughts. His memories of me obviously hadn't been tampered with, otherwise he wouldn't have said my name and agreed to walk with me. He didn't seem to be feeling anything...I couldn't stand the silence for another second.

"How are you?" I asked.

"I'm alright. What are you doing here, Kai?"

I bit my bottom lip, and slowly nodded. In that moment, I completely understood what was happening here. He was over it. He was over me. I let out a sigh and nervously fidgeted with my hair.

"I needed to know."

"What is it that you needed to know?" He asked.

"I needed to know if there was a chance for us." He stopped walking, looked into my eyes, and traced a piece of my hair that had fallen in front of my eye with his finger. The silence between us while I waited for his response was agonizing. My teeth were biting down so hard on my lower lip I almost broke the skin.

"Kai," he said, "I just……. don't think I am ready to move

on. You and I are awesome as friends, and I know we let things go further than we should have that one night, but I don't think I will ever really be over Molly. When I lost her….." He stopped talking, choking back tears, and looked down at the ground.

"I just don't think I'm ready. I don't think I will ever be ready to be with anyone other than her."

Complete panic took over. *What was he saying? Molly?* My eyes must have looked wild with anger, confusion, and what he probably thought was jealousy. His expression softened, "I'm sorry. I never should have led you on, I was just so upset and you are so incredibly beautiful inside and out. I hope we can still be friends." He hit me with a complete cliché on top of every other word of absurdity out of his mouth! My heart sank. *This…is…my…punishment. This is what I deserve.* One of three things were happening here: Madness had completely taken over my mind and I made up every memory of Lee and I, this moment wasn't real and I was really in some corner of the world going mad with guilt, or someone had compromised all of his memories of me and replaced them with false memories of Molly before she died. This couldn't be happening.

"Lee," I whispered while trying not to cry, "You have to remember. This can't be real."

"I'm sorry. I never should have led you on. You deserve better than that. We spent that last night together before you took off, and I felt like crap about it for days after. It's not like you even bothered saying goodbye when you left, or called after that, so I had to assume you realized it was a mistake too. I'm sorry if I misread something."

"I can't do this," I said, turning away from him.

"Kai, wait! Come on…..don't make me the bad guy here. I do care about you."

KAI

I waved my hand as if to bat away any more hurtful words he could throw at me, shook my head in complete disbelief, and ran as far away from him as possible.

CHAPTER

Fifteen

AFTER RUNNING FROM LEE THAT DAY, I found myself lost and completely broken. I looked around for Adrian, but he left the island. How many times can we break in one lifetime? Admittedly, I had it coming. I had all of this coming. Ava was right, the guilt and remorse finally did find me. Guilt is the worst part of every nightmare; it takes more from you than anything else in this entire universe, and never seems to satisfy its appetite. I spent what seemed like weeks lost in my own madness in the middle of the swamp somewhere literally out of my mind. All I heard were the cries and screams of the people I've hurt. I saw images of their faces as they took their very last breaths of life. At one point I honestly believed the water in the swamp had turned to blood - it was crimson red and looked thick with loss and death. The trees began taking on different forms, they were moving…coming for me. I saw their roots punch through the earth, and crawl toward me. They squeezed and strangled me without mercy. I was tangled in those sharp painful roots for days, or so I believed. Days and nights bled together as one, it was impossible to really know how long I was out there. The skies just looked violent and red. Everything was red. I begged for death. I even begged for Ava. Every time I did I could see her face reminding me she couldn't help me as long as I was on the land. I reached for my necklace, it showed me nothing. At some point, I decided if my necklace could no longer guide me the way I needed it to, perhaps I could put it to better use. I grabbed it and jerked as hard as I could against my neck. Maybe if I pulled hard enough, I'd just stop breathing. It didn't work, my pearl was meant to protect and guide me. It wouldn't even break the surface of my skin. I cried and screamed until I simply couldn't anymore. I knew I deserved whatever was coming next. Images of Liam, Aunt Morgan, Adrian, and even Lee all flashed somewhere deep behind my eyes. Somehow, all that did was make me feel worse and more alone than ever. Everything inside of me was tangled up and aching. It didn't matter who did what they did to Lee. Somewhere deep inside, beneath everything I thought I could wish away, I knew I deserved this. I was completely drowning in my own madness. Everything turned black...

Breaking waves and ambient noise had replaced the sounds of screams and the cries of my victims. Soothing azure blue water had replaced the violent red skies and swamp. I had no recollection of how I got back under the surface, nor did I care. I was home. I was laying on the bottom of the ocean floor alone. For an instant, I thought about trying to cut my tail off somehow, but I had exhausted all of my emotions. I was completely empty, at least in this moment. Peacefulness was nothing I'd likely ever feel again. It wasn't entirely unfair, but I wasn't all evil...at least I never thought of myself that way. I knew how to love, show restraint, and protect others. None if it mattered now.

"None of it matters"

"Doesn't it?" said a familiar voice.

"Liam. How did you find me? How did I make my way back down here? Have I hurt anyone?"

"Shhhh," he placed his index finger over his beautiful lips.

His finger was as smooth and cool as the inside of a perfect conch shell. "You haven't hurt anyone, Kai. Your soul is restored. I suspect the only person you want to hurt anymore is yourself." He was right. I looked up at him and let myself remember kissing him for a second. The idea of letting myself experience any sort of pleasure or momentary happiness was too much for me to handle.

"I felt your pain. We all did. I waited for you to come to the water's edge, and when you finally did I brought you down here where I knew you would be safe from your pain and yourself."

"I see," I said not really knowing what else to say. There were so many things I wanted to say to him, but now wasn't the time. I had to find a way to survive this guilt and remorse consuming my heart. "I don't remember," I said, shaking my head. Liam looked at me with love and sympathy in his eyes, "I know. You weren't making any sense. You were so…lost." His eyes told a thousand stories. I knew he never wanted me to go to the surface to begin with. He swam over to me and put his hands on my shoulders, "You did survive it, Kai. You can survive this." I nodded. The water around us was so still. The entire world under the sea was standing perfectly still waiting to see what my next move was going to be.

"I did survive it, but how do I know the guilt won't consume me again like that? How do I know I will pull myself out of it again?"

"Because I will be here to pull you out of it. You know how I feel about you. I will fight every day to keep you satisfied in our world."

"I know you would, Liam." I knew he would, and part of me wanted it so badly. Another part of me realized I could only bring him pain, and the seas only knew what else. He took my hands in his, gently kissed each of them, and made one last plea, "Please, Kai," he said. "Let me help you. Stay here with me. I will build you the most beautiful home under the sea the Gods have ever seen." I smiled, then kissed him gently on the cheek. "Would you love me and want me as much if my soul were lost again?" I asked. "Of course, I would. You know I would." I leaned in and kissed him as gently as I could, then ran my fingers through his hair. "Then I will find you. I promise." And with that I swam away from him and toward the one person I knew was sitting on her throne waiting for me.

CHAPTER
Fifteen

MAYBE YOU DON'T EVER REALLY GET AWAY with anything without paying the ultimate price. Christianity teaches people that as long as they learn to accept Jesus Christ into their lives, they will be granted forgiveness and grace - they get a ticket into Heaven. I've never quite gotten that. I don't believe for an instant that you can do terrible things, then still get a pass simply because you ask for forgiveness at the last moment. Does that mean a serial killer, like myself, could pray for forgiveness with my very last breath and get into heaven? Does anyone take curses into account? It doesn't seem likely. Other religions and cultures believe in reincarnation, the more you suffer in one life, the better off you will be in the next. Humans latch on to anything to believe in, as long as it gives them comfort, or helps them live with themselves and the evil they do. I'm immortal. I know there are many different versions of heavens and hells, and I know this is my hell. Having my soul reconnected was never going to be enough to balance the scale. I realize now if I spent the rest of my immortality doing nothing but good, I'd still be meant to suffer for all of the terrible things I've done. We are what we hide. We are all of the darkest parts of ourselves. We are what we won't let anyone else see.

This is my hell. My hell is knowing that I've lost the one thing

I've always yearned for - to be truly loved. More than that, to have finally reached a place in my existence where I was willing to risk everything to finally accept I was worthy of love from myself and from others. The last time I saw Lee, that is, when he knew who I was, he told me part of him wished he could erase me from his heart and soul. His wish was granted. The powers of the moon and the sea saw to it. Ava tried warning me that I would be punished. I just didn't understand how it might come to be. Liam is in love with me, and I have nothing left to give him as I am. This is my hell. If I am going to live my immortality in hell, I might as well be queen, and I knew exactly who I needed to see about that.

"Kai," she called in a cool clear tone. "Kai, find your way to me." Ava's words became fainter. Then the water began pushing me forward so quickly everything around me was nothing more than a whirl of blurry watercolors. Imagine swimming against a strong current and multiply that by a thousand times and tons of force. All I could do was close my eyes and allow the water to push me forward. There were no more colors, and no more sounds. There was no more fear or uncertainly. There was simply surrender, and the kind of quiet you only ever think about when you let yourself think of the end of things.

The sharpness of coral scratched my left shoulder as I was thrown against it. I stopped. I had finally stopped moving. Sand covered my tail, and crawled it's way under my smooth fingernails. I blinked a few times, shook my hair free of sand, and looked around. I assumed I'd be thrown at the foot of Ava's throne, but nothing around me was familiar - nothing but her presence. She was behind me. I couldn't bring myself to turn my head. I sat there on the floor of the ocean feeling very much like a lost child in the presence of her absolute power and self-certainty.

"My heart aches for what you had to go through above, Kai. Truly."

"Then why would you do this to me, or allow this to be done to me?" I snapped my head around and narrowed my eyes. "How could you, even you, do this to me?"

"You knew there would be consequences, a price. You paid a very high price. I am deeply sorry for the pain you must be experiencing. I can feel it seeping out of you. It covers you like a heavy cloak you refuse to take off."

"It's not as simple as taking it off, Ava. I would think you would understand that better than most."

"And I do. I also understand your cost could have been much higher. He could have been taken from this world. I went through a similar loss as well, and knowing my lost love still had a chance at life made it all a bit more tolerable."

"That and losing your soul," I snapped back at her. She looked down and smiled, "I suppose you would be right to say that." Her words stung, but I knew she was right. I was hurting, but the hurt was so overwhelming I almost couldn't tell what the core of my pain was anymore. Losing Lee was terrible. It left me with a hollow sort of feeling of despair. Emptiness…

Mixed inside of all of that emptiness was also the complete awareness of what was. I lost him. However it happened, I lost him. However Ava orchestrated all of this, it happened.

"I played no part in this, Kai," she said narrowing her eyes at me. She was reading my thoughts. "Yes, I can hear your thoughts. Even if I couldn't, I assume you would need to blame me for this somehow. I don't fault you for it, but this was the will and doing of the old ones."

"Then let me confront them," I raised myself from the ground and floated before her. "Let me go to them, let me explain…."

"That is not possible, and even if it were, I would not allow it." She swam toward me and stroked my cheek. Her presence was admittedly comforting and terrifying at the same time. I had every reason to trust her, and every reason not to. She closed her bright eyes slowly, then opened them once again to look into my eyes. "Kai, I can take your soul away - forever. I can make all of this pain go away." My heart beat quickened. "I don't think I can. I think some small part of me realizes I have to make amends for all the pain I've caused - all of the evil I've done. Redemption shouldn't be about changing for someone else. It never should have been about him. It needs to be about me. I've always known it, I just never pieced it together until now. This is something I have to do on my own terms."

"Very well," she sighed. "You must know you alerted the Old Ones with your breakdown. We all felt it, they felt it more than any other creature under the sea. You won't be safe, especially if you do not learn to channel your guilt somehow." Pictures of those lost imprisoned mermaids in that underwater hell flashed before me...

"This is why I brought you here," she said as she extended her arms out as to command me to look around. I hadn't actually looked at anything around me since I had been thrown into this place. It was so much like coming out of a coma, then beginning a conversation without a moment for anything else in between. The only thing certain about where I was standing was I had no idea where I was standing. The water was very clear. Once I focused my eyes and looked more than a few feet in either direction I began to see more coral, plants, fish, and rocks. The warmth of sunlight kissed my face and back. We were very near the surface, much too close to the surface.

"You need to leave the water for a while. You will be safe here on land."

"But…..but you told me when you restored my soul, you couldn't help me on land. Are you….Are you banishing me somehow?"

"Kai, I realize you've been through quite the ordeal, but please minimize the dramatics," she said smugly. "I couldn't banish you from the sea if I wanted to, and why would I want to?" Her voice softened again. "I've only just gotten you back. You will be safe here. It is an enchanted land. Your blood is still one of the most powerful forces on earth, all your powers are still intact, and your pearl will guide you anywhere you choose - show you anything you wish to see. There are wise creatures here, creatures you have yet to learn of, or believe exist. It is not without a few dark souls and danger, but nowhere is as long as you are on the earthly planes." I almost laughed out loud at her, "You mean to tell me you are sending off to a mythical fairy tale land to learn to deal with my guilt?" Then I laughed and shook my head, "You can't be serious. I can find a life on land among humans or find safety under the water." She shook her head, as if to agree. "Yes, eventually. Not now," she replied.

"Do not force me into a position to restore your soul with or without your consent, Kai."

"I wouldn't."

"I am your mother, and I will protect you. I also have to maintain balance and order down here. It is my gift, it is my curse. It will be your burden one day, but not today."

"I want to say goodbye to Aunt Morgan."

"It is not goodbye, and it is not possible. I cannot risk exposing you. I have cloaked this part of the water. No one can sense your energy here. You can come back under once you have adapted to everything that is." I knew she was right.

"This is not goodbye, my sweet Kai." She kissed me on the

forehead, and began to float away from me.

"Ava, wait!"

"Yes," she sang from the distance.

"What is this land called?"

"Isla."

She was gone. She was gone, and it was time for me to swim to shore.

EPILOGUE

THE SHORE WAS ONLY A FEW FEET AWAY. It was time to bring my head above water and embark upon my new journey. My fins burrowed into the sand and I pushed myself off with enough strength to scatter the sea life around me and force me to the surface. My face hit the surface first. I carefully kept my head just above the water, and looked around cautiously. What I saw was unlike anything I've ever seen, or even read about. My eyes widened and I gasped in awe. "Wow," I whispered.

New beginnings and unfamiliar places were anything but new to me. I had no idea what kind of creatures roamed this land, but I knew I could adapt and survive. This is redemption, it shouldn't be comfortable. I thought of Liam, and my promise to find him. I thought of Aunt Morgan and wished I could hug her once more before reaching the surface. I thought of the old ones, our story of creation, and the underwater hell I never wanted to see again. Then I thought about my soul, and how easy it would be to have it removed forever and take my place in the kingdom as a Sea Witch.

My story is far from over, and while this certainly isn't the way I thought this chapter would end, I know another one is just beginning.

ABOUT THE AUTHOR

 JESSICA SANTIAGO RELEASED HER FIRST PUBLISHED NOVEL, *Kai*, in 2017. She lives in Pittsburgh, Pennsylvania with her husband and two children. Jessica has always been drawn to stories about life and redemption with a fantasy twist. You can visit her online at https://www.facebook.com/peaceloveandstories/

91663868R00117

Made in the USA
Columbia, SC
19 March 2018